Cover artwork by Gombar Sanja.

https://fantasybookcoverdesign.com/

Interior artwork by Cauldron Press.

http://www.cauldronpress.ca

A huge thank you to-

Alana Ashe of Kindled Quill for Alpha Reading

Maxine Meyer for Copy Editing.

Imogen Evans for Proofreading & Editing.

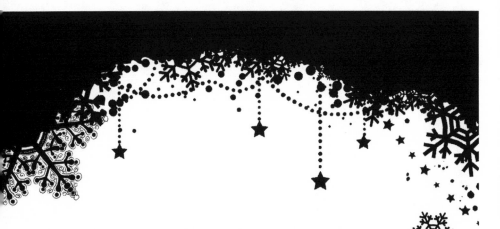

MISTLETOE
MATES

SEDONA ASHE

CONTENTS

Chapter One

—CANDI—

L et's have a Christmas hunt, they said. It will be fun, they said. What 'they' didn't say was who they planned to hunt... or what the prize would be.

Oh yeah, that would be *me* on both accounts. Even though the temperatures were near freezing, cold sweat still tricked down my spine.

Wolves howled in the distance. Their calls were savage, the sounds of untamed beasts having caught a scent. My scent. They had to be close now.

Crap on a Christmas cookie! How had my night taken such a nightmarish turn?

One moment we'd been having a wonderful Christmas Eve dinner. The next, my father stood, announcing there was to be a mate hunt. Hunts were great fun, and they were something our entire pack enjoyed. But a mate hunt hadn't been held in several decades after the female wolves had joined together and threatened to leave the pack if these hunts continued.

Men cheered, howling in excitement and eager to bring back the archaic tradition. My stomach churned for the girl they would be hunting, and at the turn the dinner was taking, foreboding settled around me like a dark cloak.

My father waited for the hoots and howls to quiet down a little before announcing that the prize the men would be hunting... was me. In shock, my glass dropped to the floor and shattered into a million pieces while my heart did the same in my chest.

I opened my mouth to protest, to say that I would rather eat twenty pounds of fruitcake than be hunted and given as a prize to the winner. But my father turned his unrelenting, dark gaze to me, his white brows lowered over his frosty eyes, and I knew I didn't stand a chance. The alpha's word was law. To defy him in front of the entire pack would be a quick way to be turned into a rogue.

The room erupted in chaos, the men practically drooling over the prize being dangled in front of them. *Me.* I gagged, unable to breathe through the testosterone choking out the oxygen in the room. The men, whose attention I'd turned down countless times before, were beyond thrilled at the chance to take me, the alpha's daughter, as their mate—the ultimate Christmas gift, all the while their eyes sparkling with what they probably thought was Christmas spirit.

For as long as I could remember, my father, Alpha of the Evergreen pack, had been obsessed with all things Christmas-related. He saw himself as a weird werewolf version of 'Santa Claws.' It was as though he believed if he failed to trump his Christmas celebration from the year before, the very magic of Christmas would die.

He was delusional, and as such, everything in our pack revolved around the holiday theme. It didn't help his obsession that the pack's primary source of income came from the near-endless busloads of tourists who traveled to visit Evergreen during the winter months.

The pack houses were reminiscent of the adorable cottages from a German Christmas village, each adorned with intricate trim and twinkling lights. All the trees surrounding the homes were covered in cheery decorations.

Our quaint town offered gingerbread house building contests, warm apple pies with hand-whipped cream, steamy cups of decadent hot cocoa, reindeer sleigh rides complete with jingling bells, steep sledding hills, epic snowball fights, and rich meals by the enormous stone fireplace that covered one entire wall of the dining hall.

Oftentimes, guests would visit several days in a row to enjoy everything our little town offered. They loved the experience and hated to leave the magic of Evergreen. All the while, our guests had zero clue that the creatures they were celebrating Christmas with were creatures far better suited to Halloween—werewolves.

"Please, Dad," I whispered under my breath.

His white scruffy jaw set. "Know your place, Candi."

Oh, I knew it all right. From the very moment I was

born, I'd been little more than another tool for my father to use in promoting his insane love of Christmas. I just never thought he would take it this far. I had underestimated him, and tonight had proven that fact yet again. His obsession with his persona mattered more to him than his own daughter.

The thought of it made me want to roll my eyes, or sob, but unfortunately, I couldn't do either since my eyes had all but frozen solid during my hasty escape.

My father had only given me a fifteen-minute head start. It wasn't to give me time to gather any supplies or things I might have wanted to take with me. No, the head start had simply been a way to further excite the male wolves and drive them into a greater frenzy.

I didn't have many earthly possessions, mostly because I preferred a simple life without a lot of fuss. But my heart ached that I'd been forced to leave my mother's jewelry, her journals, and the small trinkets she had bought me when I was a child.

My mother passed away when I was six years old, and her belongings were the only things I had left of her besides my memories, and I treasured each one. I suspected my father didn't give me enough time to gather them because he hoped it would ensure my compliance with his newest game. He wanted to keep my mother's things as insurance that I'd return rather than run away for good.

He was fed up with me. Over the past few years, I'd made it crystal clear I wouldn't take a mate unless he was my soulmate. I longingly dreamed of finding that perfect mate, no matter how small the odds were that I'd find him. Soulmate matches were rare among werewolves, but not impossible.

My father had pushed relentlessly for an arranged marriage. He'd hoped to wed me to one of his strongest wolves, but each time, I'd declined. Now, it seemed father dearest had finally grown tired of waiting for me to find my soulmate and decided to take matters into his own hands.

While my father held the male wolves back, giving me the minuscule head start, it was barely enough time to grab my boots and my jacket before I rushed out into the snowy evening. The pack had murmured in excitement as they watched me bundle up, and cheered when I disappeared into the dimly lit woods. The very idea of me trying to outrun these men while in human form was absurd, but I had to be in human form for my ill-conceived plan to work.

I was brought back to the present when a shadow seemed to dart between the trees. In my panic, I missed my footing and stumbled. I fell to my knees in a deep snowdrift, losing valuable time. And right now, I needed every single precious second.

The night echoed with the Evergreen wolves' eerie howls, much closer this time. Too close.

Hurry. Hurry. Hurry. I chanted the words in my mind, trying to push myself harder.

Night had fallen as I escaped the woods and ran across snowy fields. I tripped again, my half-frozen legs giving way as I collapsed to the ground. Grinding my teeth together against my current discomfort, I scanned my surroundings.

At first, I couldn't make out anything in the darkness, but eventually, I spotted an old mansion in the distance. Its deep mahogany paint and intricate gothic-style woodwork were a stark contrast to the brilliant white snow that lay in soft billows around it.

I froze as the reality of what I was about to do sunk in. Time was running out, but was I truly ready to risk a confrontation with the Brimstone pack? They were just as likely to turn me into a rug for their hearth as they were to listen to my pathetic plea.

Blowing on my numb, blue fingers to warm them, I tried to come up with an alternative. Any alternative would be better than the bleak option in front of me.

There was none, and the howls were closer than ever before.

My eyes burned with unshed tears, and I bit back a scream of frustration over the unfairness of my situation. I wasn't just up the creek without a paddle. No, this was more like skydiving without a parachute and praying some stranger would be willing to catch you.

I blew out the breath I'd been holding and pushed myself forward on trembling legs. There was no more time to think. It was time to act or succumb to my fate. I ran through the deepening snow, tripping and falling multiple times as I made my way toward the dark, imposing house.

I would've been able to cover the distance between the two packs in half the time if I'd been in wolf form, but that wasn't a safe option. Under werewolf law, a shifter in wolf form who was found on another alpha's territory could be executed instantly, with no repercussions.

While it was rare in modern times for most alphas to actually take advantage of this rule, it wasn't a risk I was willing to take. Especially not when it came to this particular alpha. The Brimstone Alpha wasn't known for being friendly and had garnered a reputation for being brutal when dealing with trespassers.

And that is why I stayed on two legs, even though it made me slower and I was freezing my butt off. I was hoping the alpha would pause long enough to consider showing me mercy rather than killing me on sight.

Forget about the werewolf romance novels where the alphas were all friends—or at least got along well enough to visit each other's parties. That was fiction and not the world I lived in. In reality, alphas were cutthroat and brutal when it came to any wolves not in their pack. This forced our species to live inside stiff pack boundaries and follow rigid laws.

Male werewolves, regardless of rank within a pack, were excessively territorial over what belonged to them. As long as every pack stayed within its boundaries, our species was able to avoid a full-on war.

And I'd just crossed the boundary into the Brimstone pack's territory.

My only hope was that Coal, the Brimstone Alpha, would accept me into his pack and decide not to kill me. If Coal accepted me into his pack, I would be considered his, and his alpha nature would drive him to protect me. Hope was free, wasn't it?

Unfortunately, my father and the Evergreen pack still considered me their property, and from the sounds of how close the male wolves were, they didn't plan on giving up anytime soon.

Surely, they wouldn't come onto Brimstone land, would they? It would be a serious risk, and for what? Female wolves weren't rare; there were plenty of eligible females in the Evergreen pack. They would risk starting a war if they continued to hunt me on another pack's land.

Running up onto the porch, I grabbed the icy cold doorknob and instantly regretted it when my sweaty palm stuck to it. I twisted hard, but the heavy oak door held fast. After peeling my hand off the handle, I darted around the side of the house. I found a small side door and yanked wildly on the knob. Again, the door held fast, locked up tight.

Not ready to give up, I ran to the back of the house. My hands shook as I grasped the aged bronze doorknob with both hands and twisted. Surprise, surprise. It was locked. With full-blown panic creeping through my chest and clawing at my lungs, I tried the knob once more. This time, I shoved my shoulder against the massive wooden door. It didn't even budge.

I fought the urge to scream out my frustration. If I cried out or knocked on the door, it could alert the wolves hunting me to my location, so I pressed my lips together and stayed silent. The situation was dire. I'd never felt so helpless, and it wasn't a feeling I liked.

Please. Please. Please be home. Twisting the knob again, I mentally begged for anyone to answer the door.

There was no response. I'd thought facing a member of the Brimstone pack would be terrifying, but it turned out that no one being home was worse. The fear I had been holding at bay swelled up and threatened to overwhelm me.

I had to find the alpha before the Evergreen wolves found me. Alpha Coal either needed to accept me or kill me. Otherwise, my only other option was ending the night being hauled back to Evergreen as someone's prize... and that option wasn't an option at all.

The wind changed direction, and a fresh scent blew my way. The wolves from my pack were here. I'd run out of time and out of luck. My gaze darted around the porch and yard, searching in vain for somewhere to hide. Spotting an ancient trellis trailing up the house, I practically threw myself at it and began scrambling up toward the roof.

It was not the smartest move, but in their wolf forms, the men would have trouble following me. They'd have to be complete idiots to come onto Brimstone's land in their wolf forms. In the past, their brains had proven to be about as useful as a hedgehog in a condom factory, so they might be dumb enough to risk trespassing. Especially if they thought the numbers were in their favor.

Halfway up the creaking trellis, I slipped. My face slammed hard against the side of the house. The rough wood boards ripped skin from my cheek, but with the adrenaline pumping through my system, I barely registered the pain. My fingers were frozen stiff, making it much harder to grasp and climb. After several more slips and near falls, I finally clambered onto the snow-covered roof.

Looking down, a wave of dizziness washed over me. The house was only two stories, but werewolves aren't exactly known for our love for heights. I didn't get much time to freak out over the height, though, because movement in the tree line caught my eye. My neck snapped in that direction, and I quickly flattened myself on the rooftop.

A hint of familiar black fur darted between the trees, and my stomach, which had been free-falling toward my numb toes, changed directions and launched itself into my throat. Remaining still and not daring to even breathe, I prayed my pack wouldn't find my trail. Maybe they would give up and disappear back into the forest...

A wolf emerged from the thick pines and stepped into the clearing. As the wolf was bathed in the pale moonlight, I recognized the midnight black as Evergreen's pack beta, Randolph. I couldn't believe the arrogant butt-sniffer would risk his life just to win this hunt. Actually, maybe I could believe it. Randolph had always thought himself above the rules, and he had a habit of pushing boundaries when it came to me.

Sadly, it didn't take long for the beta to catch my scent. His victorious howl filled the frosty night air, sending a chill that had nothing to do with the cold skating down my spine. Fear propelled me back to my feet with the overwhelming need to escape.

Deep down, I knew that if I couldn't hide here, there was nowhere else I could go. Nowhere I could run to find safety.

Stumbling along the old mansion's snow-covered roof, my temples throbbed as I tried to figure out my next move. There was no way I could outrun the male werewolves, not even if I were in my wolf form. I was fast, but not faster than those who had been viciously training for years.

Up on the roof, I was out in the open. The werewolves hunting me wouldn't immediately think to search above them, but the moment the wolves looked up and caught sight of me, it would be game over.

Amid my despair, frostbite, and rising panic, I tried to think of an escape route. Anything was better than sitting here waiting for the inevitable. I refused to stand here while my chance of finding my soulmate was stolen from me. I was worth more than ending up as the winner's prize in my father's twisted game.

That was when I spotted the chimney surrounded by snowdrifts on the roof.

There was no elfin' way I was going down a chimney.

Nope. Never. Not happening. There was a better chance that the real Santa Claus would show up and travel down that chimney.

There had to be another option.

Chapter Two

—CANDI—

Please let there be another option. *Please.*

Blowing on my frozen fingertips, I glanced at the clearing surrounding the house. The wolves were swiftly closing in on me. They were nearing my tracks, and once they found those tracks, I'd only have minutes before they realized I was on the roof.

I glared at the chimney through narrowed eyes. What if I tried to slide down it, only to break my neck? That still sounded better than having one of the wolves below claim me with a mate bite. I'd be alive, but my soul would be dying a slow death with each passing day.

As quietly as I could, I tiptoed to the chimney. This had to be the stupidest idea I'd ever come up with. I probably wouldn't even fit! For all I knew, they had a fire going. *Fine.* I knew that was a lie since there wasn't any smoke curling out of the chimney, and the bricks beneath my hand were colder than ice cubes, but that still didn't make this a good idea.

Scrubbing my hands down my face, I struggled with my jumbled, chaotic thoughts. Perhaps I should just return to my father? Maybe I could hide in my room until this ridiculous hunt was over. But would I be able to beat the pack of wolves hunting me back home? If I did make it, would my father declare me the winner if I returned home by myself, or would he just repeat this fiasco again? I swallowed a bitter, hiccupping sob, already knowing the answer. He would probably pick a male from the wolves and declare him the winner, and allow him to mark me.

I scooted my butt onto the top of the chimney, mentally preparing myself to begin a careful descent. My movement dislodged the snow, sending it sliding off the roof in an avalanche. The thick sheet of snow hit the ground with a muffled thud. It was the type of sound a human may not have noticed, but there was no way it would have escaped a wolf's sensitive hearing.

The beta wolf's head snapped toward the roof. His glowing, hunt-crazed eyes traveled along the mansion's roof. I didn't think he had seen me yet, so I did the only thing I could.

I dove headfirst into the chimney. Belatedly, I prayed I wouldn't break my neck. For the first ten feet or so, I banged along far too fast. The rough bricks skinned my elbows, shoulders, and my already sore cheek. I choked back my cries of pain.

The chimney grew tighter, slowing my descent until I

was able to use my raw palms and knees to stop my dizzying fall. It was a relief, since I was less likely to break my neck if I could control my landing.

Inch by inch, I worked my way down the dark walls of the chimney.

That was when it happened.

I was thin, but my mother had blessed me with a juicy peach, if you know what I mean. Wait a minute, who am I kidding? She may have given me the genes, but my love for donuts and hot chocolate had certainly helped with the rounded shape of my booty.

Long story short, I wasn't meant to be squeezing down chimneys.

To be brutally honest, I didn't think anyone but Santa was meant to be squeezing down chimneys.

My body was kicking up ash and soot, making it hard to breathe in the tight space. Blood rushed to my face, and a wave of dizziness washed over me. Tears dripped from my eyes while I nearly suffocated from the effort of trying to breathe but not cough.

I sucked in every bit of my body that was suck-in-able while simultaneously wiggling the rest of my body like a belly dancer—or, more accurately, an uncoordinated cater-pillar on speed. It seemed like forever, but finally, I saw the opening of the chimney below me.

I huffed out a relieved breath, which dislodged my body and sent me slipping fast down the last few feet. My fall came to an abrupt halt when my hips became firmly, and painfully, wedged in the chimney... stopping me four feet from the floor and leaving my head and shoulders dangling in the open fireplace hearth.

Wiggling back and forth, I tried to free myself, but it was no use. I couldn't dislodge myself.

"Ugh!" I half-groaned and half-cried at the same time.

Reaching up, I tried to get a fingerhold on the bricks to push myself up. When that didn't work, I looked around, searching for something I could hang onto while pulling myself free. There was nothing within reach, and the bricks were far too smooth to grip. I was helpless to free myself, and I cursed the beautiful, perfectly glazed donut I'd eaten that morning. This day couldn't get any worse.

The open fireplace hearth was spotlessly clean, like it hadn't been used for a while. That would have practically been a sin in the Evergreen pack, where the sound of crackling fires filled every home and most businesses.

This was a grand fireplace, like something from a wealthy country estate in old England. It was easy to imagine the elegant dinner parties that were probably held in front of this imposing stone mantle many decades ago.

Squinting, I tried to bring the rest of the room into focus. This was difficult since the heavy curtains were drawn shut, and the large room was lit by only one small lamp. As my eyes drifted around the dark room, I came face-to-face with a set of wide, shocked, heart-stopping blue eyes.

Santa's sleigh! At that moment, it hit me just how terrible my idea had been. In my desperation to escape the Evergreen werewolves, I'd imagined knocking on the front door and begging the alpha to accept me. I hadn't thought of how terrible it would look for me if I was caught breaking and entering... and I was definitely caught. There wasn't a snowball's chance in Hades the alpha would show me mercy now.

The blue-eyed man cleared his throat. "Um, Coal? I think you forgot to call the exterminator. It looks like we have another pest in the chimney."

I heard a man's frustrated sigh, clearly missing the underlying tone of shock in his friend's voice, but I couldn't find him in the shadows of the room. "The company said they would come back out to block off the chimney, but that was over a week ago. I'll call him again tomorrow."

"Okay." Blue-eyes dragged the single word out over several syllables. Tilting his head, he studied me with a taunting air as his lip twitched up. "But what are we supposed to do about this one? It's too big for the dustpan, and I think it's stuck."

"Well, I dealt with the last one, so this one is yours to deal with, Frost." Coal's voice echoed from the darkened corner of the room. "I left the welding gloves on the side table. Make sure you don't get bit. It could be rabid."

My fear of this pack and its reputation was so ingrained and powerful that I'd forgotten to breathe. Thankfully, my heart had remembered to keep beating, although it was hammering against my ribs with a force that promised I'd be sore later. All that changed with Coal's dismissive comment about me biting.

I gasped, outraged at being treated like an animal. Well, I was one, but not the kind they were talking about. He was taking things a little too far, and my anger shoved my fear aside as it surfaced. The rush of blood from my fury was followed by another wave of dizziness, reminding me I'd been upside-down for too long.

When Blue-eyes, a.k.a. Frost, reached for the thick protective gloves with a grin on his face, the last tendrils of my self-control snapped.

"Oh, come on! Surely you aren't being serious! You can clearly see that I'm not a squirrel or raccoon!" Belatedly, I added, "And I don't have rabies!"

There was a derisive snort from the shadows. "Be careful with it, Frost. It sounds angry."

He was right about that! It—er, I—was furious. Coal had every right to kill me for trespassing, and I accepted that. What I couldn't accept was being treated like a mindless animal. If he planned to kill me, he could at least let me maintain whatever scraps of dignity I still possessed. All right, fine. I probably only had a single tiny scrap left. But that wasn't the point.

I squirmed and wiggled, covering myself in more black ash, but still not freeing myself. A wolf's howl sounded outside, followed by several others. I stiffened. My anger vanished as terror consumed me. Even with all the blood in my body pooling in my head, I turned pale as a ghost.

"What do they want badly enough to risk their lives by trespassing on my land?" Coal snarled.

That... would be me.

Holding my breath, I couldn't have spoken up if I'd wanted to. Frost crossed the room and bent in front of me until our eyes were nearly level. Up close, he was shockingly handsome, and I took the opportunity to memorize his every feature from my upside down position. His short dirty blond hair was quaffed to the side in an easy style that seemed to echo his teasing personality. He ran a huge hand along his scruffy square jaw and tapped a finger against his full lips in an overly dramatic way. There was no way his lips were as soft as they looked, right?

"I don't know, Coal." Frost lifted his brow, and his eyes drilled into mine, appraising me. "But I think our little visitor does. Don't you, Pest?"

Pest? Who did he think he was to call me that? My jaw clenched with the desire to snap my teeth in a warning for him to back off, but it would probably convince him to use the welding gloves when freeing me. That would've been the humiliating icing on an already awful day. I jerked as the wolves howled just outside the house, the hair-raising sound draining all the fight out of me. This wasn't the time to get my panties in a bunch and lose my temper. I needed to let go of my pride and beg for my stocking-stuffing life.

Unable to stay still while knowing I was trapped and the Evergreen wolves were only feet away, I began to struggle, not caring that I was causing my skin to tear and my body to bruise. "Yes, I do know. They're after me. Could you please help me get free?" I hated how my voice cracked on the word 'free,' and I hoped Frost wouldn't catch it.

Frost's blue eyes narrowed. Why were his eyes so pretty? And were his eyelashes white? "What do you mean they're here for you? More to the point, why are *you* here?

We aren't exactly welcoming to visitors, especially not if they come from the Evergreen pack." The way he said my pack's name told me everything I needed to know about how he felt about us.

Hold your sleigh bells. I stopped struggling.

"I don't understand. How'd you know I'm from the Evergreen pack?" Werewolves didn't wear a visible mark showing which pack we belonged to, so how could he have possibly guessed my pack?

Frost tapped the side of his nose and gave a soft smile that did something weird to my heart. Although, it was just as likely my heart was acting up because it was having trouble pumping blood through my upside-down body.

Frost leaned forward slightly, and I was spellbound as he took a deep breath. "Pest, you smell like the living embodiment of Christmas."

Time was running out, and I needed Frost's help. I decided to try a different tactic. I batted my eyelashes and relaxed my lips, trying my darndest to appear seductive. "Please, Frost. Help me."

Frost fell back on his heels, laughing until he clutched at his sides. "Coal, man. I can't do this." He wiped the tears from his face, and his eyes sparkled with mischief.

Frost's reaction would have been a blow to my ego, but being stuck upside down in a chimney must have robbed me of the ability to feel much worse about myself. Instead, I crossed my arms and huffed.

From the shadows stepped the second man. I knew Coal by name only, having heard the whispered tales of the alpha and his exploits for many years. He wasn't a man known for kindness, nor was he known for being social. It was rumored he never left his house unless there was an issue in his pack he needed to address, or he was forced to visit the Elders.

And I'd just entered the sanctuary of his home like I was the big boss straight outta the North Pole... minus the red velvet suit and the whole getting stuck part.

Chapter Three

—CANDI—

C oal moved across the floor without even the slightest whisper of sound. Every cell in my body screamed for me to run. He was a dangerous predator, in both his human and wolf form. With his short dark hair, tight beard, and tan skin, he looked like a dangerous shadow moving rather than a man.

His chocolate brown eyes shifted to obsidian as they traveled across every part of my body that was visible with a look I couldn't quite decipher. "Are you here to spy for the Evergreen pack, little wolf?" Coal's voice was simultaneously as smooth as honey and as sharp as a blade.

I'd never admit it out loud, but my body instantly responded to him. Blood tried to rush to my lady bits, but that wasn't happening in my current position. My body flushed, and a sheen of sweat covered my skin. This made no sense, and I struggled to understand the unfamiliar things I was feeling. He was handsome, but all male wolves tended to have movie star good looks, and I never reacted to another male like this. So why was my body desperately desiring this stranger in a way I'd never experienced before?

Get it together, Candi. This wasn't part of the plan.

"N—no." The word came out a stutter, a sign of weakness I despised. Clearing my throat, I met his eyes and tried again. "I came here to join your pack."

Coal's eyebrows rose almost to his dark hairline. "Every werewolf pack on earth knows I rarely accept new members into my pack. Why would you come here knowing my answer would almost certainly be no?"

I could hear the wolves howling at each other as they circled the mansion. Shouldn't Coal be doing something?

"They're trespassing! Why aren't your guards stopping them? Why aren't you ripping them apart? I would've expected the alpha of such a powerful pack to have better security. But apparently, you just let anyone wander onto your property nowadays." I waved my hand at myself. "Case in point."

Frost cackled, causing Coal to shoot him a disapproving glare that would've had most wolves cowering. Instead, Frost gave a careless shrug of his shoulder. "Sorry, man. She's funny."

I huffed. White spots danced in my vision, and I was fairly confident I would pass out if I didn't get out of the chimney ASAP. "I'm a whole lot funnier when I'm not upside down. I'd really like to get down now. Please."

Curling his lip in disgust, Coal focused back on me. When he spoke, his voice was low and lethal. "I've known you were on my property from the instant you stepped onto it. The only reason you are alive is that I was bored and thought some entertainment would be nice. You delivered that in spades. Now, listen carefully, as I won't repeat my question a third time. Why are you here?"

"My fa—alpha." I'd been about to say *father*, but doubted that would score me any points at this crucial moment. "Is a bit obsessed with Christmas."

"I am well aware." Coal didn't look amused, which definitely earned him points in my book. I'd happily take a grouch over a wannabe Santa any day of the year.

I kept my eyes locked with Coal's, even though my wolf was screaming for me to look away from the alpha. "Yeah, well. Tonight, to kick off his Christmas celebrations, he decided to have a mate hunt." Tears burned the back of my eyes, but I refused to show how deeply I was hurt by my father's decision. I blinked rapidly to keep the tears at bay.

Frost and Coal shared twin expressions of shock at my revelation. After an awkward pause, Frost spoke, his voice vibrating with anger. "Are you telling me there are female wolves running around the dark woods in below-freezing weather, being chased by horny males looking to claim them without courtship? The Evergreen Alpha is allowing females to be hunted for sport?"

"Yes. Um. I mean. No." I hesitated. My gaze dropped from their faces, not wanting them to read my expression. "It's just me."

"Just you?" Frost asked in disbelief, pushing to his feet.

"Yes. Only me." My voice sounded pitifully small, even to my ears.

Coal took a sharp step forward, and I automatically jerked back at his sudden movement. Catching my reaction, Coal paused mid-step. "I won't hurt you."

His words were gentle, and my heart ached in response. Being this close to the powerful alpha must be messing with my head. It was the only explanation for how he was affecting my emotions and body with nothing but his voice.

Coal had a reputation for being dangerous and having little mercy. My father constantly warned our pack about the dangers of anyone from Brimstone catching us. But none of that fit with the man in front of me.

"We can continue this discussion after she is out of our chimney. That can't be comfortable, and her face is turning an alarming shade of red." Frost moved toward me, but Coal held out an arm to stop him.

"If we pull her, it could injure her or cause her hip bone to break. I'd prefer to avoid that. It's best if she tries to free herself first." Coal warned.

Once he was satisfied Frost wouldn't interfere, Coal grabbed a chair from an antique side table. Sliding it beneath me, he was careful to keep his movements slow and unthreatening.

Bracing my hands on the back of the chair, I was able to push myself up a few inches. It was just enough for me to wiggle and un-wedge myself from the position I'd been stuck in. The moment my hips were free, I tumbled face-first toward the chair. Thankfully, my wolf's instincts kicked in. I managed a sloppy half-flip, landing in an awkward heap on the chair. It was far from elegant, but at least I wasn't stuck any longer.

I sighed in relief at being right side up and rubbed my face, trying to ease the headache building in my skull, no doubt smearing more soot across my pale skin. It was something I'd worry about later. Now that I was free and sitting in front of the Brimstone Alpha, it was time to do what I'd risked my life to come here for.

I needed Coal's help, and it had to happen now. If I wasn't a part of his pack, and under his protection, before my old pack knocked on Coal's door, then by the werewolf bylaws, I could be claimed as Evergreen property and taken back to my father's pack, where I'd be forced to wed the beta who was bound to say he'd found me first.

"Alpha Coal. Please, accept me as a member of your pack," I blurted out. "There's no way I can outrun those wolves, and I can't imagine a life where I lose the right to choose my mate, and I'm bound in marriage to Randolph, the beta."

Coal and Frost blinked at me, neither man under-standing how absolutely desperate I was at that moment.

Swallowing the tattered remains of my pride, I sagged to my knees in front of Coal. "I can't be mated to him."

"You do realize, even if I claim you as a member of my pack, they could argue I didn't have enough time to make it official. In that case, you would still be under the Evergreen Alpha's rulings." Coal's voice was rough, but not cruel.

How was it possible for my heart to sink and soar at the same time? Coal hadn't said no. He was contemplating accepting me as a member of his pack. But he was right. I'd forgotten there was a chance they'd still have a claim to me. Under werewolf law, an alpha could kill intruders on the spot without repercussions. If the wronged alpha decided not to deliver immediate punishment, then the offending werewolf would be returned to their pack, and their alpha would be responsible for any further punishment.

These rules were in place because the Elders didn't want werewolves living indefinitely as prisoners in tiny cages or cells. When a werewolf was unable to shift into their wolf, they'd slowly lose their minds. It was a cruel death.

As the alpha, Coal could kill me immediately for trespassing, but by showing me mercy, my pack could try and claim the right to drag me back to Evergreen and punish me there. Accepting me as a pack member might not be a strong enough claim for Alpha Coal to keep me.

A sob caught in my throat. I might be forced to return to Evergreen.

For some inexplicable reason, the idea of leaving these two men sent a sharp pain through my soul. What was it about them that made me want to run my hands through their hair and taste their lips? Why did spending the rest of my life trying to make them smile sound like heaven instead of hell? I'd never felt this way about anyone, ever. Certainly never about the Evergreen Beta.

A shudder went down my spine. I didn't want to be my father's pawn for the rest of my life, and I couldn't allow myself to be married off to the man who had spent a better part of his life making me miserable. Sure, he'd changed the past two years, but only after my figure started becoming more pronounced, and he realized that marrying me put him in line to become the next Alpha of the Evergreen pack. At least with the men in front of me, I was making a choice for myself and not letting my father decide my fate.

Coal dropped to one knee. Not a position for an alpha. "Look at me."

Hesitantly, I tilted my face up to meet his.

His voice was rough. "What would you be willing to do to become a member of my pack? Just how far would you go, little wolf?"

Chapter Four

—COAL—

I 'd resigned myself to spending another cold winter day reading while simultaneously trying to ignore Frost's incessant jokes and attempts to annoy me. It hadn't been going well, and I'd been mentally begging for a distraction. The universe must have taken pity on me. After all, it wasn't every day that a beautiful woman dropped through one's chimney upside down.

I was more than a little intrigued. Our guards had informed us the instant the she-wolf had stepped onto our land. The first person who dared to do so in years. My curiosity had piqued, and rather than shifting and rushing outside, I'd waited to see what the female would do.

The she-wolf's pounding on the door to be let inside had been surprising. The decision to run across my roof? Well, that was interesting but had been strange. Having her come face-first down the chimney? Now, that had been completely unexpected, and I'd been instantly intrigued.

Her arrival filled the room with the intoxicating fragrance of spicy cloves, smokey cinnamon, bruleed sugar, and a hint of pine. She smelled of Christmas, a holiday I hadn't celebrated in years. Although, if I'd known Santa Claus looked like the beautiful little vixen hanging upside down in my fireplace, I'd have reconsidered my stance on not celebrating the holiday, and Santa could have come down my chimney when she pleased.

I want to make her come every night of the year. Where had that thought come from? Shaking my head to clear it of the lust clouding my mind, I knew exactly where it had come from. My normally aloof wolf's interest had been stirred by our visitor's arrival. I started breathing through my mouth, trying to avoid inhaling more of her intoxicating scent, but that just led to it sliding across my tongue in an even more distracting way.

Normally, I would've ordered Frost to drag the trespasser out of the chimney and toss her outside on her perfectly rounded butt. Instead, I'd wanted to help her down myself. The urge to touch her skin had been all-consuming, but I'd seen the fear in her eyes when I got too close.

For the first time in my life, I wanted to curse my reputation as the boogeyman of the werewolf world. To everyone outside of my pack, I was an evil, cruel, Christmas-hating villain who preferred killing people rather than talking to them.

Frost snorted, giving away that he'd been eavesdropping in my head.

Okay, fine. The last part was true. I despised endless small talk and mindless chatter, but I tried to be mostly fair about my decisions regarding who lived and who died. That should count for something.

So, what was it about this blonde-haired, green-eyed female that had me utterly captivated? Was it her beautiful, heart-shaped face? Was it the tangle of long, soot-covered blonde hair cascading toward the floor like a modern-day Rapunzel?

Maybe it was the way she'd gotten flustered when we'd pretended she was vermin. Her irritation at our continued teasing had been glorious and rare for an outsider. I couldn't wait to tell our kids about it someday.

Hold up. Kids?

Loud howls from just outside my home were a welcome distraction from the strange turn my thoughts had taken, and I turned to study the unusual female. Her shoulders were drawn up to her ears, and she was biting at her thumbnail.

My werewolf hearing easily picked up on the harsh pounding of her heart. She'd been gutsy when she dove headfirst down the fireplace chimney, even knowing she'd have to face the dreaded Brimstone Alpha if she survived. Now, anxiety rolled off her in palpable waves. The strange thing was that anxiety didn't seem to be caused by me, which is what I would have expected. No, her agitation was caused by whatever, or whomever, was outside my door.

I hated it, and I hated that the emotions this stranger was feeling bothered me. It made no sense. I'm supposed to be a villain. People left villains alone. It was a role I'd always been content in. Hadn't I?

"Please, accept me as a member of your pack. There's no way I can outrun those wolves, and I can't imagine a life where I lose the right to choose my mate, and I'm bound in marriage to Randolph, the beta."

Slipping off the chair, she dropped to her knees at my feet. "I can't be mated to him."

Horror coursed through me. She shouldn't be on the floor, nor should she ever have felt the need to kneel in front of anyone and beg. I swore everyone who'd made the little she-wolf this terrified and desperate would pay with their lives.

"You do realize, even if I claim you as a member of my pack, they could argue I didn't have enough time to make it official. In that case, you would still be under the Evergreen Alpha's rulings, and they could force you to return with them." I bit back a snarl at the thought of her being dragged away from me.

There was one option, and it was one that my wolf approved of. My stomach twisted in disgust at what I was about to do. In her eyes, I was probably going to turn from her would-be savior to a predator taking advantage of her dire situation.

I dropped to one knee in front of the trembling she-wolf. I ignored Frost's gasp of shock at my action. An alpha never kneeled in front of anyone.

"Look at me," I ordered, still fighting against the desire to touch her soft, milky skin.

Slowly, she raised her face to look at me.

I dropped my mask and let her see the obsidian of my soul. There was a part of me that wanted to scare her away so she wouldn't accept my offer. She deserved so much better than this.

"What would you be willing to do to become a member of my pack? Just how far would you go?"

She looked at me with teary green eyes. "I want what I've never had. The chance to make choices about my own life. Tonight, I chose this pack, the Brimstone pack, as my pack. I am choosing to leave the Evergreen pack. Please. Fight for me. I'll do anything if you can find a way for me to stay here."

The trust in her expression was a punch to my gut and caused my hardened heart to crack. It'd been countless years since I'd felt much of anything, so finding out I still had a heart was surprising. I'd always done my duty and taken care of my pack, but my life lacked any real joy or emotion.

My wolf, who was relatively passive, paced in my mind with the insane urge to help her. For all I knew, she could be a threat to my pack. But why then would my soul be screaming with the need to protect her?

The door shook as fists pounded against it, and the blonde lurched toward me, instinctively seeking my protection from the Evergreen male wolves who had no intention of leaving my territory without her. Her skin barely missed touching mine. My wolf's incessant demand to touch her pounded in my skull.

"I'll be right back." My words were a low rumbling promise, or perhaps a threat?

I strode to the front door, pushing aside my newly discovered emotions and preparing to meet my extremely unwelcome guests. Violently throwing open the door, I snarled at the five men standing on my porch. "You better have an unbelievably good excuse for trespassing on my land."

Wanting to ensure they knew who they were talking to, I released a pulse of alpha energy. My canines lengthened, and my eyes began to glow. It was a warning to the trespassers of how thin the ice was that they were standing on. My reputation might be exaggerated, but it was based on truths. I could snap their necks without emotion or exerting myself.

For several long moments, the men stared in open-mouthed shock. It was a reaction I was used to. No one spoke. They were wasting my time.

"I'm waiting," I growled, pushing more alpha command into my tone. It forced them to take an involuntary step back from me, which pleased my wolf. He was on edge, and if I didn't get them off my property soon, things were going to take a violent turn—which wouldn't necessarily be a bad thing. I had a lot of energy that needed to be released.

"We've tracked one of our pack members to this location. It appears she accidentally trespassed on your property. We're here to take her back and apologize for any inconvenience she may have caused you. You know she-wolves can be a bit dense when it comes to werewolf law." He shrugged at the last part and curled his lips in a tense grin.

Did the idiot seriously think we were going to bond over his misogynistic views and disrespect toward female wolves?

Eat him. My wolf licked his snout.

I suppressed a shudder and tried not to wonder what deeds my wolf might have done when I was in my were-wolf form, and he had control.

"Leave now." I began to shut the heavy wooden door.

The male stepped forward and used his foot to keep me from closing the door. My gaze slid down to his foot, then back to him. He gulped, knowing he was on dangerous ground. "Alpha, we can smell our female in your home. If you would just send her out to us, we would be on our way. There is no need to kill her. Our alpha will see that she is punished, and after tonight she will wear a tighter leash."

The female took a sharp inhale.

Paint the snow with his blood. The beast in my mind was shaking with rage.

It took every bit of control I possessed to keep my voice even when I spoke. "I'm well aware. The she-wolf has requested to become a member of my pack. I've accepted her request. She is now a member of the Brimstone pack, which means she's no longer any concern of yours. Leave now." This time, I let the full force of my alpha tone vibrate through my words.

All the men dropped to one knee and averted their gazes... all except the beta male. He shifted his gaze to the doorframe beside my head but refused to kneel. A low growl rumbled in my chest. Insolent pup.

The stubborn beta cleared his throat. "I find it unlikely she has switched packs so quickly. How can we be sure you're not holding her here against her will? She belongs to the Evergreen pack, and she needs to return with us. It would be a shame if the Elders had to become involved in sorting this out. I'm sure they have better things to do than deal with a disobedient she-wolf."

My eyebrows rose. Was this beta actually questioning me? It was laughable and irritating. By werewolf law, I was well within my rights.

Was it frowned upon to kill other werewolves? Yes. But was I within my rights to execute trespassers? Yes. Did I purposely cultivate the image that I was cruel and that I enjoyed executing people? You bet.

People were far less likely to visit if they believed you might kill them for stopping by with a fruit basket. You'd never catch people knocking on my door. Want to sell me a vacuum? It will help clean up your scattered remains. Hand me a free booklet warning of my eternal doom? I'll help you find your eternal peace a little sooner.

The main obstacle I faced if I wanted to keep the she-wolf was the Elders. They frowned upon keeping hostages. We could kill trespassing werewolves but keeping a were-wolf in captivity was considered cruelty of the highest degree.

To avoid long-term prisoners, the Elders created bylaws allowing a pack to reclaim their lost member. If a pack came looking for their stray pack-mate, and the alpha hadn't already executed the trespasser, the pack had the right to take back their wandering wolf. Which meant the men on my doorstep could stir up trouble for me with the Elders.

I didn't care. They weren't taking the adorable chimney-sweeping she-wolf from me.

Not now, not ever.

Someone better come by to sell me a vacuum soon. By the looks of things, I was going to need it.

Chapter
Five

—COAL—

Before I could stop her, the female squeezed by me. Blondie was careful not to touch me, but I didn't miss the way her body leaned toward me while staying out of the reach of the beta male. Interesting.

She trusts us. My wolf preened.

I gave an internal scoff. *Doubtful. She fears us less.*

It was odd, considering I was considered a monster among wolves.

She trusts us to protect her. The beast in my mind was all but gloating.

The woman addressed the beta. "Randolph, I'm no longer part of the Evergreen pack. Alpha Coal is speaking the truth. This is where I wish to be. Tell my father I wish him the best for the Christmas holidays." Her voice was hard, not giving away even a hint of fear.

The beta, Randolph, took a harsh breath. "You don't mean that."

"Yes, I mean every word. It isn't exactly a secret that I've been unhappy for years. You know that better than anyone." There was a bitter edge in her tone.

Turning to look up at me, she gave me a whisper of a smile. "Alpha Coal accepted me as a member of his pack, and this is the fresh start I've wanted. He's been exceedingly gracious in his dealings with all of us stomping all over his territory, so I'd suggest you five return to the Evergreen territory before his hospitality runs out."

I wasn't sure what to make of this situation. She was backing me up, and I was getting the distinct impression she wouldn't mind seeing me rip into these wolves.

Crossing her arms under her chest, she lifted her chin in defiance. She was a force to be reckoned with. "He doesn't like guests on his porch," she tried again when the wolves made no move to leave.

I bit the inside of my cheek to keep from laughing out loud. The little minx made me sound like a mentally unstable, crotchety old man. Worry pierced through my amusement. Was that how she saw me? A mean old fart?

Unacceptable. Take her to the bedroom and fix this. My wolf growled, beginning to pace again.

My mind conjured all types of ways I could change the way she saw me, and my body grew hard. Why was she having this type of effect on me?

The beta wasn't ready to give up. "Until this can be sorted out properly and the correct paperwork is filed, you're required to return to Evergreen. The Elders can discuss your transfer, but you will return home tonight… with me. It's not your decision to make, Candi."

Candi. Her name was Candi. It was disgustingly adorable… and it suited her perfectly. Would her lips taste like candy?

I pulled my thoughts back to the current situation and pinned Randolph with a predatory gaze. He was treating Candi as though she were a naughty child, but the flare in his eyes said he definitely didn't see her body that way. The four men behind him nodded in agreement. None of them were bothered by the way the beta was speaking to her, so this likely wasn't something new. Possible reasons for why she'd run to my pack started to take shape.

They may have been allowed to treat her with disrespect on Evergreen land, but they had no right to boss her around while they stood on my land.

"This is my land, my home, and you are standing on my porch." *Great. I was reinforcing the old man vibes.* "You will not order Candi around or speak to her with disrespect in my presence." Without thinking, I slipped my arm around her waist, tucking her close against me and away from the Evergreen wolves.

The movement caused my hand to slide beneath the edge of her shirt. My fingers brushed against the velvet-soft skin of her waist. Electricity sizzled through me with enough power to nearly send me to my knees. It was a once-in-a-lifetime surge that every werewolf dreamed of

43

experiencing. My mind was struggling to comprehend what my body had already figured out...

Candi was my mate.

I'd given up looking for my mate long ago. I'd never dreamed she would come down my chimney. Joy, shock, elation, desire, and fear twisted inside me until my emotions were in a tangled mess. My wolf wiggled his furry tail in what I thought was a weird little dance. He was relieved to have found his soulmate—his other half.

Randolph stepped forward, grabbing her arm. With a rough jerk, he attempted to yank her away from me. Wrong move.

My wolf lunged in my mind, and I fought the shift. I wanted to rip Randolph's throat out, but killing a beta was a lot more paperwork than I was in the mood to fill out. It would mean I'd have to leave my newly found mate and report to the Elders immediately.

Thankfully, Frost saved me from my indecision. Frost emerged from the shadowed doorway with a vicious growl. His feral rage caused the hair on my body to stand on end. Frost, a laid-back wolf with near-perfect self-control, was fighting against his shift. It was unsettling, to say the least.

My always present third in command, Aspen, stepped from behind the tall hedges surrounding the old mansion. His large red wolf snapped its jaws and circled the porch steps.

"I'd suggest you withdraw your hand and step back. NOW." My voice shook as I fought my wolf for control. "You are three seconds away from losing that limb."

The Evergreen Beta took a reluctant step back, his face hardening into the expression of a man ready to fight over the thing he wanted. Tough luck, I wanted her too. I'd wanted her from the moment her cute little butt got stuck in my chimney, and now that I knew she was my mate, nothing on earth was going to take her from me. He was a strong beta, but he didn't stand a chance against me.

"You can't just claim Candi as part of your pack! There are rules, and you know it! Turn her over now, or you risk starting a war between our packs." His nostrils flared with barely contained anger. "Besides, what makes you think you have any right to claim her?"

Slipping a second arm around Candi's waist, I pulled her tighter against me, nestling her in my embrace. She might kill me for it later, but right then, I didn't care. The female wolf had already made it clear that she'd do anything to be part of my pack and stay out of the clutches of these ravenous men.

My wolf rumbled happily when Candi leaned her full weight against me. Turning her head, she rubbed her cheek against my shirt, and her pupils dilated when she inhaled my scent. She wasn't running scared; she was letting me hold her. I wondered if Candi even realized her wolf had made a subtle claim by brushing her scent on my shirt.

Mate likes us. Don't ruin this, old man. It was hard to take my wolf's warning seriously when he was happily wagging his tail like a dang golden retriever.

Resting my chin on top of her head, I flashed my teeth at

45

the Evergreen wolves. It was a threat, not a friendly smile, and they knew it. "Candi is my mate."

Her body stiffened in my arms, but she played it cool. A few seconds later, Candi relaxed and leaned her full weight against me. She'd accepted my touch and didn't deny my claim that we were mates. My wolf was euphoric, and my heart soared.

Randolph barked a harsh laugh. "You've got to be kidding me! Are you really going to try convincing us that you happened to find your mate today? I know you're lying. Candi is *my* mate. I might not be able to take her back to Evergreen with me today, but I'll return with the Elders."

He leaned toward me, baring his teeth. It was a bold move for a beta. "Keep your hands off her, or there will be war. Candi. Is. Mine!"

Rage roared through me at his claim. Since they were on official pack business, the Elders wouldn't be pleased if I killed them, but their ire had never stopped me in the past. The only thing that kept this arrogant jerkoff alive was the fact I was holding my mate in my arms. I wanted to spend the next few days learning everything I could about her, not stuck in endless meetings with ticked-off Elders.

Candi bristled, no doubt preparing to fire back at him.

Mentally, I willed her to stay quiet. He was testing me. It delighted me to see her fire when we'd teased her about being a rabid pest, but I needed these men off my territory before I lost control of my temper and my wolf. The moment they had touched her, he'd been fighting to shift and rip these men to shreds. I wanted the same, but this wasn't the time.

I held my breath, waiting to see her reaction. Instead of speaking, Candi shifted in my arms. Wrapping her arms around my waist, she rested her cheek against my chest and smiled up at me. She'd effectively dismissed the men, treating them as if they were no longer there while at the same time turning her back on dangerous males to face me.

I wanted to smile at her blatant show of disrespect toward the beta and haul her to the bedroom for being willing to turn her back to them, trusting I would protect her, but I managed to keep my features neutral.

"Frost. Aspen. Handle this. I'm taking Candi inside to warm up." I didn't wait for them to respond before stepping backward through the doorway.

Frost had gained control of his wolf and casually leaned against the railing, his trademark smirk on his lips. Aspen gave a thunderous bark and snapped at the Evergreen men.

As soon as I shut the door behind us, I stumbled against the wall, dragging Candi's soft body to me. My breath was coming in rough pants, and my wolf howled to be released. Unfamiliar sensations were wrecking my body and confusing my mind.

"Why did you tell them I was your mate?" Candi's eyes held worry and something else I couldn't put my finger on.

"Because we are. I didn't know for sure until I touched you. Didn't you feel the pull of the mate bond when my hand touched your skin?" I ran a finger down her cheek, unable to keep myself from touching her.

47

There was no way a wolf could miss the lightning bolt that shot through them when the mate bond activated. Candi had to have felt it. She'd rubbed her scent on my shirt and surrendered herself to my embrace. I watched the realization dawn on her tired face. Candi had felt it, but she hadn't fully understood what 'it' was. Had no one explained to her how it felt when you found your soulmate?

Stretching on her tiptoes, my beautiful mate raised a trembling hand and brushed it along my stubbled jaw. My skin vibrated everywhere Candi touched me. Between the threat to my mate from the Evergreen wolves and her touch kicking my hormones into overdrive, my wolf was losing his mind with the need to mark her.

With a strength I didn't know I possessed, I forced myself to remain still, letting her fingers explore my face for several long minutes. My self-control cracked when the scent of her desire reached my nose, and she lifted her dilated eyes to meet mine. Unable to stay motionless, I slipped my hand through the silky veil of her hair to the back of her neck and cradled her head in my palm.

"I want to kiss you." My voice was hoarse and unrecognizable as my own. Gone was the self-assured werewolf alpha, and in his place was a nervous puppy who'd do anything for the woman in his arms.

Her eyes glittered with tears. "Then kiss me, Coal."

That was all I needed to hear. Bending down, I brushed my lips along hers with a featherlight touch. I groaned at the feel of her body melting against mine. The heat of her curvy body seemed to scorch my skin and send my body into overdrive. How had I gone from planning to live out my life as a bachelor, to desiring this she-wolf more than I'd wanted anything else in my life?

I devoured Candi's mouth, her sweet taste hitting me like the world's most powerful aphrodisiac. Using my grip on her hair, I pulled her closer and tilted her head to give me better access. I didn't want any space between us at all.

Vaguely, I heard the squeak of the door opening behind me, but I was too lost in the velvet brush of her tongue against mine to care. Frost tried to squeeze by us in the narrow entryway but ended up bumping into Candi's hip.

Candi gasped into my mouth.

Frost froze.

I moaned at the loss of her mouth as she pulled away from me to stare at Frost with wide, green eyes. Even through the blood pounding in my ears, I could make out the thundering of her heart and her ragged breathing.

"What's going on?" I demanded, not too pleased about being interrupted. Why wasn't Frost giving us privacy? He liked to mess with me, but this was not the time.

Frost took a step toward Candi, his hand outstretched. My wolf was too close to the surface and too territorial over his mate to allow another male to touch her. A growl tore from my throat.

To my utter shock, Frost's eyes snapped to mine and hardened. He snatched Candi, hauling her against him. With a snarl, he flashed his elongated canines in challenge.

The werewolf world knew Frost as my beta. What they

didn't know about my childhood friend was that Frost was a blood-born alpha. Not wanting to leave the pack and wanting to keep our friend group together, he'd chosen to act as my beta—something unheard of for an alpha. This was the first time he'd ever challenged me or defied a clear order to back down.

If this had been any other situation, I would've stopped to ask him what was going on. But Frost was holding my mate, who was filling the room with the scent of her desire, and my wolf was seconds away from forcing my shift.

Clenching my jaw, I took a step toward him and reached out a hand for Candi. Frost shoved her behind his back, his muscles rippling as he fought his own shift.

He'd moved my mate out of my line of sight. Frost was keeping her from me, and now he'd die for it.

I lunged for Frost.

Chapter Six

—CANDI—

"**W**hoa! What the—" A red-haired giant with a thick beard barreled between the growling men. Grabbing Frost's shoulder, the giant tossed him into the door with the flick of his wrist. And with a hard shove of his shoulder, he knocked Coal back against the wall with enough force to cause a dent in the drywall.

Before I could blink, the newcomer swept me off my feet and cradled me against his chest. He seemed ready to haul me out of the situation. He was powerful, and I wouldn't have been able to escape his embrace if I'd wanted to. Warm tingles sizzled across every nerve ending in my body as a third mate bond activated. The man's body turned to stone. He didn't twitch or even take a breath.

"What is going on? This makes no sense." Was I going to

create a mate bond with every male werewolf who touched me from now on?

Wolves had a single mate. One. So how did I have three? Dropping my head against his chest, I willed this to be a super freaky dream that I'd wake up from any minute.

"Mate?" The red-haired man said the word as a question. He sounded almost as perplexed as I was about our current situation.

"Mine," Frost growled, pushing away from the door.

The giant turned, using his broad body to shield me from the other two guys, neither of whom looked pleased.

"Aspen. Give her to me. She's my mate. You heard me claim her as my mate in front of the Evergreen Beta. Candi felt it too," Coal ground out, his hands clenching in tight fists when Aspen's massive hand patted my back in reassurance.

"That may be. But she is my mate as well. So, we have a problem." Aspen stroked a finger down my hair. "Why are you covered in ash, beautiful? What did they do to you?"

Before I could answer, Frost pushed away from the door, shoving his hands in his pocket. He was agitated and struggling to remain calm. "She's my mate."

How does this happen? Could this day get any more confusing? I had just escaped a pack of men looking to claim me as their mate, only to end up with another pack of men trying to claim me. Was there something in the air other than Christmas?

"This isn't the time for your jokes, Frost." Coal shot him a withering look before taking a step in Aspen's direction.

I expected the red-haired wolf holding me to back away from his alpha. Instead, Aspen puffed out his chest and stood taller, bracing himself to fight Coal.

Frost stalked toward us. "Who's joking?" His voice had dropped to a dangerously low pitch that vibrated through the room.

"You're both wrong. She's my mate." Aspen's arms tightened around me, and his muscles tensed.

I needed to do something to defuse the situation, but what?

Think, Candi, think.

This evening had been one crazy twist after another, and I was struggling to adjust. My mind was exhausted, and my body needed sleep. But I'd never been the cowering type. With a speed that surprised everyone, including myself, I wiggled free of Aspen's hold and slid down his body to the floor.

Rushing between the three men, I held up my hands. "Okay. Everybody, calm down. There's no need to—"

I didn't get any further before Aspen cut me off. In one smooth move, he grabbed me around the waist and swung me to the top of a tall cabinet as though I were a toy they needed out of the way. The instant I was safely out of harm's way, the men charged at each other, and the mansion shook with their furious growls.

This wasn't one of those friendly fights where they pulled their punches and messed up each other's hair. Oh no. My ears rang with ripping fabric, the thud of fists and kicks connecting with skin, and muffled hisses of pain. Coal hurled Aspen into the cabinet beneath me. I shrieked in fear as the cabinet tottered from side to side, threatening to send us both crashing to the floor.

"Frost! Coal! Aspen!" My cries and angry shouts fell on deaf ears. The men hadn't even shifted, but they were far too lost to their wolves to hear me.

Glass shattered as Frost went flying into a table, where Coal leaped on top of him. Aspen grabbed Coal and flung him away from Frost, only to turn on Frost himself. Coal landed on his feet and, without breaking stride, raced across the room and launched himself on Aspen's back.

I could just keep sitting here like an elf on a shelf, or I could do something to stop this before they killed each other. But I wasn't an idiot. Getting between three male wolves as a human would have been a death wish.

If I shifted, I'd be quicker at dodging punches, and any injuries I sustained would heal faster. Still, getting between them in my wolf form was only slightly safer than my human form, but it was the best option I had at the moment.

"Can't believe I have to do this," I muttered under my breath, removing my soot-covered shirt and setting it aside.

I quickly removed the rest of my clothing without the men even noticing. They were fighting over me, yet none of them noticed I wasn't wearing a single stitch of fabric. It would've been laughable if I wasn't so irritated by the ridiculousness of the situation. Why couldn't we talk this over like rational adults? Instead, they were at each other's throats.

In one fluid movement, I leaped off the top of the high cabinet and shifted effortlessly into my wolf. With a bark, I rushed into the fray, nipping limbs… and maybe a cute butt or two. I blamed my wolf for that.

Confused, the men whirled around, searching the room for the new attacker. With them no longer fighting at a blurring speed, I was able to see them clearly. Worried they may have hurt each other, my eyes darted over their bodies, taking stock of their injuries… until my body warmed, and I was nearly panting.

Deck the halls! These guys were ripped to the point of being carved from stone. During the fight, they'd torn each other's shirts and pants, and the garments hung in tatters from their sweat-covered bodies. Through the gaping holes, bulging muscles flexed and rippled. Trying to be discreet, I licked my wolfy lips and hoped they hadn't noticed my drool. These men couldn't truly be mine, could they?

"Candi?" Coal asked.

I cocked my head to the side as if to say *yes?*

Eyes narrowing, Coal looked down at the holes in the seat of his pants. Holes that had been left by my sharp canines. Oops.

Aspen choked on a laugh. "She bit you, Coal!" The crazy red-haired man grinned at me, pride shining in his eyes. "You are a gutsy little thing."

It was more like I'd just proven I was a few lights short of a Christmas tree. Biting your alpha was a quick way to meet your end. Deciding I needed to show I was sorry, even though I'd enjoyed biting him, I dropped to my belly and scooted toward him. Giving him my best sad puppy eyes, I whined pitifully.

Coal gave an exasperated sigh, then bent on one knee to stroke one of my silky ears. "Don't do it again. Got that?"

I licked Coal's hand and wagged my tail, thankful he couldn't read my thoughts. If he could, he'd know I absolutely planned to do it again. And again.

Frost burst out laughing, and we all jerked around to watch him warily. "Candi! I get it! Candi, like a candy cane!"

I rolled my eyes, already knowing where this was going. Frost ignored me and continued to cackle.

"Aspen, look at that cute little red swirl around her tail," Coal cooed. Yes, the big bad wolf, Alpha of the Brimstone pack, actually *cooed.*

Coal sat back on the ground and pulled my wolfy body onto his lap like I was a pet pupper. Which I absolutely wasn't. No, I was a freaking terrifying werewolf. I huffed at the disrespect, expecting my wolf to rip Coal's hand from his body and beat him with it. Instead, she whined and rolled over for tummy rubs.

I was horrified.

Werewolves didn't really enjoy being petted in their wolf form, yet Coal had my wolf begging for attention. Chest rumbling with sexy laughter, the alpha scratched my stomach. Completely embarrassed, I decided I was never shifting back to my human form.

"I've never seen anything like her pelt," Aspen whispered.

Their reactions weren't a surprise. My wolf form always garnered this response. I dropped my snout onto my paws. Coal's hands stroked my body, running along my shimmering white fur. My coat had a glittering effect that the pack doctor had enjoyed studying. He'd finally learned that the individual hair follicles were constructed like fragmented crystals. This allowed light to shine through the strands and create a sparkling effect.

Coal's fingers scratched behind my ear, finding that spot I never could reach. I swished my fluffy white tail and heard Coal's soft chuckle. Cracking open an eye, I caught his amused expression as he studied the red fur twisting around the puffy white fur of my tail... exactly like a candy cane, as they said.

I'd been born with the delicate crimson ring around my tail, and my father saw it as proof the moon goddess approved of his fanatical obsession with all things Christmas. Growing up, he'd drilled into my head that I was a sign the moon goddess favored the Evergreen pack. That was all I'd ever been to my father. A token and a trophy to show off.

I should've dyed my fur green to see what dear old dad thought about that.

"It's adorable." Aspen must have sensed the depressing turn in my emotions and was trying to reassure me that my unusual marking didn't disgust him as it did me.

My heart melted. When was the last time anyone cared about my feelings? I gave Aspen a wolfy smile, and my tail thudded softly against the hardwood floor. Leaning down, he brushed his long fingers through my fur, and I stiffened in surprise.

After my mother died, I hadn't experienced affection. The only times I'd been touched were when I was being bullied. I was so touch-starved that the idea of cuddling with my mate or being held while I slept, caused my heart to ache with longing. My eyes drifted closed, delighting in the touch of my mates... even if they were only petting my wolf.

Chapter
Seven

—CANDI—

Frost stood and walked to the cabinet to gather my clothing. Bringing them to me, he placed them on the floor in front of me. "Come on, Pest. Time to shift back so we can talk."

Pest? I growled and snapped at his hand. Frost only laughed and gave me a quick tap on my nose. I stared at him in slack-jawed horror. Please tell me he did not just 'boop my snoot.' I was going to kill him. With two backup mates, I could afford to lose one, right? But what if I left the room and the other two started fighting? Tilting my head, I studied each man for signs they might lose control.

"Stop worrying, Candi. We're done," Coal reassured me. "We'll step into the living room to give you privacy. There is a bathroom down that hallway."

I grasped the clothes in my powerful jaws and made my way to the bathroom. Shifting easily, I hurried to yank on my clothes. I was surprised to discover I didn't want to be away from the guys, not even for a few minutes. Except Frost. He was in the were-doghouse.

Not bothering with my shoes, I padded back down the hall in my socks. Entering the living room, I paused and tried to assess my reaction to each man. I needed to know for myself if they truly were mine or if my body was spazzing out from my heightened emotions. Walking to Coal first, I leaned down and pressed my cool palm against his face. Tingles raced along every nerve ending in my hand.

When we'd been on the porch, my adrenaline and fear were so high that I hadn't initially recognized my wolf's reaction to Coal's touch. It wasn't until he slipped his arm around me and told Randolph I was his mate that the full realization slammed into me.

This whole night seemed impossible. How strange that I ran from a mate hunt because I didn't want to be mated, only to end up running into my fated soulmate.

Reluctantly, I stepped back. Coal reached for my hand to pull me into his lap. Smiling, I shook my head and dodged his hands. Still ignoring Frost, I moved toward Aspen. His heavy gaze was fixated on me with a mixture of trepidation and hope. I sat on the arm of his chair and brushed the back of my hand along his jawline.

Aspen's hand slid up my arm, caressing my skin. Everywhere his fingers touched, my skin hummed to life and static popped. I had zero idea how this was possible, but there was no doubt that both Coal and Aspen were my mates.

Sighing, I pulled away and strode across the room to stand in front of Frost. Instead of looking guilty, his blue eyes sparkled with barely contained mischief. He was trouble, and I secretly loved it.

Before I even laid my hand on him, I knew exactly what I would feel. Sure enough, the instant our skin connected, the electric sizzle of the mate bond zapped across my skin.

While both Coal and Aspen had allowed me to walk away, Frost did not. His hands wrapped around my waist, hauling me onto his lap so that I straddled him.

"Hello, beautiful." I wanted to stay mad at him, but Frost's sexy rumble was turning my stomach to jelly. It wasn't fair.

"Hi." My voice came out breathy, and my cheeks flushed with embarrassment. What was wrong with me? I'd never given a guy a second look, and now I had three fated soulmates. I took a quick peek around the room. Three really, really hot mates.

Before I could stop myself, I asked the question we all had to be thinking. "How is this going to work? Can it even work?"

Several long moments passed where the guys were obviously carrying on a mental conversation, one that I wasn't privy to.

Finally, Coal answered me in a steady voice. "We didn't plan for this, but we will figure things out. We've shared everything else for the better part of our lives, so the moon goddess giving us one mate to share shouldn't have been a surprise. It will take some work, though. Werewolves don't share, and they are territorial over their mates. Which means there will likely be some jealousy we'll need to deal with. But we're in agreement. You are too important to us, and we aren't willing to walk away."

Tears blurred my vision. They wanted me, and they weren't going to leave me. We'd figure out this weird situation we'd been tossed into, and everything would be okay. I had a real family. Never again would I have to feel alone.

Frost pulled me against his chest, patting my back awkwardly as I tried to stop my tears. His hands slid up my neck, capturing my face between his calloused palms. Gently pulling me forward, his lips pressed softly against mine. Fireworks exploded, and my lips moved on their own, hungry for more.

Frost didn't hesitate, and he matched my enthusiasm as our lips danced. Unable to help myself, I trailed my hands up his chest and across the frayed remains of his shirt, enjoying the feel of his skin against my palms.

Frost groaned into my mouth. "I can't believe I found you. I searched for so many years." His hands moved to explore my body, running along my waist and teasing across my breasts. I arched my back into him, wanting and needing to feel his touch everywhere.

"You didn't exactly find her," Coal cut in, his breathing harsh. Without being able to see his face, it was difficult to tell whether it was from irritation or desire.

"No, she found us when she tumbled down our chimney." Frost kissed the tip of my nose. "Cutest Santa Claus I ever did see. It makes me regret that we didn't celebrate Christmas these past few years. Maybe she would have come down our chimney sooner."

"I think Christmas is my favorite holiday now." Aspen chuckled from somewhere behind me.

"It's definitely my favorite holiday now," Frost agreed, his hands slipping beneath the hem of my shirt to rest against my bare skin.

The simple touch set off a wave of desire so strong I struggled to breathe. "I hate Christmas," I gasped.

"Oh, do you now? I think we'll need to do something to change your mind," Frost whispered against my ear, his warm breath sending a rush of heat straight to my core.

"I agree," Coal added. Moving silently across the room, the alpha sank to his knees behind me. He pressed his lips against my neck, and his fingertips teased up my spine.

Having both men's hands on me at the same time was more than I could handle. I moaned, unsure whether to lean forward into Frost or arch back into Coal's chest.

"Kiss him," Coal murmured in my ear, and my body rushed to obey him. I leaned forward, and Frost's lips captured mine again. The kiss shifted from sweet to steamy real quick.

Frost's right hand slid up higher, tickling across my ribs before cupping my tender breast through my bra. I'd never hated an article of clothing as much as I hated my bra at that moment. I longed to feel my mates' skin against my skin, with nothing between us.

Coal's hands trailed across my back to rest on my hips. Grasping me firmly, he pushed me forward until the evidence of Frost's desire pressed against me. Unable to help myself, I wiggled. Frost groaned with pleasure and dropped his head back against the top of the chair.

"Be still." Coal growled the order, nipping at my neck with his teeth.

Who knew being bossed around could be such a turn-on? I certainly didn't.

Biting my lip, I fought the desperate urge to shift my hips against the massive bulge in Frost's pants. Just when I thought I'd spontaneously combust, Coal rocked my hips forward and back. The movement was excruciatingly slow, and I trembled at the overwhelming sensations that were building inside me.

Frost's thumb slipped beneath the band of my bra, caressing the sensitive underside of my breast. His lips caught mine in another passionate kiss, all while Coal's mouth licked and nipped a trail up my neck. They were going to kill me. I'd escaped my pack, only to die of lust.

What a way to go, though.

Coal grabbed the hem of my shirt, lifting it over my head. The cool air did nothing to stop my skin from flushing with a mix of embarrassment and lust. I wanted these men more than I'd wanted anything in my life before. I'd gone from never being touched to having multiple sets of hands stroking and touching me. It was creating a desperation in my chest as my body threatened to come unglued.

"I've never heard of a werewolf having more than one mate." My voice was little more than a breathy whisper.

"Neither have I." Coal nipped my neck. "I'd prefer to have you all to myself, but I would never deprive you of your mates. The moon goddess knows what she is doing, and at least she picked two males I can tolerate." I could hear the mocking smirk in his voice.

"Right back at you, jerkwad." Frost huffed, speaking to Coal, but refusing to stop tasting my lips.

Twisting around on Frost's lap, I searched the shadowed room for Aspen. I needed to know he was willing to give this—*us*—a try.

Aspen's eyes glowed a warm topaz hue, showing his wolf was just under the surface. "I'm not the type of man to share, but for you, I'll learn to adjust."

A cloud of butterflies took flight in my stomach, and hope bloomed in my chest. I never thought I'd find my soulmate, let alone three mates who wanted me. It was overwhelming, but also amazing. I'd nearly given up on the dream of one day getting my happily-ever-after.

Frost's left hand had joined his right, and he continued to tease my breasts. I swallowed a needy whimper when his fingers slid further into my bra. With shaking hands, I tried to unclasp my bra, only to be stopped by Coal.

"Let me help with that," Coal offered. He removed the bra and let it drop to the floor. "Why stop there?" Reaching around my waist, he unbuttoned my jeans.

It took some wiggling, but we managed to get my tight jeans off. That's when my current situation sank in, and I began to tremble. I was straddling Frost in nothing but a thong, while two men touched my bare skin, and a third watched.

"I expected red underwear with Christmas trees or reindeer, but dang! Your tiny black thong is sexy!" Frost's voice held a teasing note that eased my sudden nerves.

I playfully narrowed my eyes at him, feigning annoyance.

"Ignore him, love," Coal spoke between placing kisses up my back.

Frost rocked his hips, causing delicious friction against my sensitive heat. Biting down hard on my lip, I barely avoided moaning out loud. Frost continued rocking his hard length against me until both our breathing grew ragged. My thong was soaked through, and I blushed, knowing I'd probably left a wet spot on Frost's jeans as well.

"Lift her up, Coal," Frost growled, his voice strained.

Coal didn't hesitate. With one smooth move, Coal stood, lifting me off Frost's lap, except it wasn't to settle me back down on Frost's length. Nope, he was keeping me out of Frost's reach.

I yelped at the sudden shift in altitude. Ignoring my reaction and Frost's curses, Coal turned on his heel and headed toward the staircase.

Chapter Eight

—CANDI—

"Coal? Wait!" I gasped, trying to squirm free of his hold.

My blood had turned to molten lava, and my body ached to be filled. I was a little irritated and a whole lot frustrated by this abrupt interruption.

Without breaking stride, Coal flipped me over his shoulder as though I weighed nothing. His hand smacked my bare butt, and I squeaked in surprise at the slight sting.

"Behave." Coal's deep voice held a teasing tone, with a hint of his alpha tone leaking into the word. The alpha tone didn't work on me, so I continued to wiggle. I doubted Coal even realized he'd given me a command at all.

"Hold up, mister! You can't tell me what to do." *Except in the bedroom*, I added silently to myself.

Coal paused mid-step at the top of the staircase.

"Why'd you stop?" Confused, I glanced around, curious as to what had caused him to stop dead in his tracks.

"I… I don't know." Coal kept one arm wrapped around my thighs, keeping me balanced over his shoulder. With his free hand, he rubbed the back of his neck.

Impatient, I started wiggling again. Games were fun, but my wolf was growing impatient. We needed our mate. Like, yesterday.

Shaking his head as if clearing a fog, Coal moved toward a door at the end of the hall. He kicked it open with his foot and carried me inside. Twisting as much as I could, I studied the room. There was no question who it belonged to. This was Coal's den.

The walls had been painted a deep, smoky gray. A large black rug was spread haphazardly on top of the dark mahogany floor. My gaze landed on the bed sitting right smack in the middle of the floor, and my eyes widened in shock at its massive size.

A black satin comforter lay messily across the bed and partially pooled on the floor, revealing the crimson sheets beneath it. The bloodred sheets were the only pop of color in the room, and they created a stunning effect.

Everything about this room oozed seductive masculinity. Coal's hand brushed my bare butt, his fingertips teasing my wet heat and sending electricity firing through my body. I wanted him. My canines ached—my wolf wanted him, too. Who needed a bed this big?

"What took so long?" I jerked in shock at Aspen's voice.

Searching the dim room, I found my red-haired mate

reclining on a dark leather recliner. His eyes roved my body with a hunger that thrilled and terrified me.

"This isn't a show!" My skin burned, and my voice cracked. The man was a freaking giant, how had he snuck by us to get into the room? "How'd you even get in here?"

"Our wolves need time to adjust to the stress of sharing a mate. Eventually, we may be able to allow each other to have individual time with you, but for now, it's best for all our sanity if we stay together." Aspen tucked his arms behind his head.

His powerful muscles rippled with the change in position, causing me to suck in a harsh breath as my body reacted instantly. Thanks to the three hotties, I'd gone from level-headed prude to thirsty ho-ho-ho ridiculously fast.

"Plus, Coal crashed my time with you, so I'm absolutely going to return the favor." At Frost's voice, I jerked in Coal's arms and clutched my chest. With an unapologetic laugh, Frost blew me a playful kiss from where he lounged on a large black velvet sofa near Aspen's chair.

How had they even gotten in here? I glanced at the dark curtains covering the windows, but they seemed undisturbed. It made no sense.

"I should have nailed my closet closed when I had the chance," Coal grumbled.

Aspen chuckled and spun a broken lock on his finger. "You'll need a new lock for the trapdoor. This one seems to have broken. Such a shame."

Coal sighed. "You two can stay, but for the love of all things horror, shut up, or I'll kill you." Coal delivered the threat in a flat tone that left me questioning if he was joking.

Tossing me onto the bed, Coal removed his sweats so fast that my butt was still bouncing on the mattress when he crawled up the bed toward me. I don't know what I expected. It wasn't like I had any experience with sex, but I definitely wasn't prepared for Coal's target-like focus.

Coal used his body to pin me against the mattress. "Candi, I am barely hanging onto my wolf. It is taking every bit of my strength to keep him under control, but there's a chance he might break free. I wish I were strong enough to walk away from this until I was in full control, but I can't. You are my mate, and I intend to claim you as mine while you are screaming my name."

Coal's words should have sent me screeching into the night like a deranged Christmas caroler. I was inexperienced when it came to sex, but even I knew that playing hide the candy cane with a barely restrained werewolf was a bad idea. Especially when it was your first time. But I couldn't make myself leave, no matter the risks.

My wolf whimpered, sensing how close Coal's wolf was to the surface. After years of waiting for our mate and spending the past several hours terrified we would wake up connected to a wolf who wasn't our soulmate, she was desperate to be marked by his wolf.

"I'm a wolf, not a glass ornament, Coal." Reaching out my hand, I patted his cheek in an awkward gesture that was meant to be reassuring. "It'll be okay."

Coal leaned forward and pressed his forehead against

mine. "Any woman who would throw herself down a chimney and jump into the middle of a werewolf brawl is one tough lady. In my life, I've experienced far more loss than joy. It's safer to keep to myself rather than risk the pain of heartache."

I didn't miss the way Coal's eye slid away from me, or the way his lips tightened.

Staring blankly at the wall, the Brimstone Alpha continued. "Once I stopped caring, the pain of losing, or being betrayed by, those I'd do anything for stopped bothering me. Fate made sure I learned the hard way that people often only seek out my company for the advantages that come from knowing me, not because they value actual friendships."

I caressed the rigid muscles in his biceps and felt my heartbreak at the pain dripping from his words. No wonder he had retreated from the public and kept to himself. Anger simmered in my chest, hot and demanding. I wanted to hunt down everyone who had dared to hurt this beautiful man. My man.

My mate.

Yes, mine. My wolf rumbled. *Bite now, hunt later.*

Despite my rage, her thoughts made me want to laugh. We were both ready to stake our claim. Coal was ours, in all his broken perfection.

Coal turned his glowing eyes and studied me. "I don't know if I can ever learn to trust again. And with time, I've grown to prefer the quiet of my home and enjoy how people avoid me."

71

He seemed to believe what he was saying, but there was no hiding the raw loneliness in his voice.

"We'll figure it all out, Coal. The most important thing is, we have each other... and Aspen and Frost." I leaned forward to place a soft kiss on his lips, craving the taste of his mouth.

Coal's lips captured mine, kissing me with a wildness that warned of the coming onslaught of his need. When he pulled back, my mouth was swollen, and we were both panting.

"I never thought I'd have a mate. You're a gift, Candi." His voice had deepened, his vocal cords growing rough with lust.

"A Christmas gift?" I teased, unable to stop myself.

Coal groaned and caught my mouth in another searing kiss. It was meant to shut me up, and I made a mental note to find ways to annoy him in the future just so he'd be forced to shut me up... often. He didn't seem like the type to enjoy punny jokes, so maybe I should try that first.

I lost my train of thought as Coal's tongue teased across my bottom lip, demanding entrance. Liquid desire burned through me.

"Oh, Coal!" I moaned, arching my body into his.

"I may not like Christmas, but I've always enjoyed licking candy canes," Coal teased as his mouth moved from my mouth and down my neck. His hand danced along my skin, trying to memorize every curve of my body.

Fumbling a bit, I reach between our bodies to grasp his

thick manhood. I gave him a hesitant squeeze, smiling delightedly when he jerked hard in my hand.

"Yes. Touch me." Coal hissed through his teeth. Wrapping his hand around mine, he slowly moved my hand along his length. His body shuddered, and his breathing was harsh. "Don't stop. I never want you to stop."

If I'd thought I was turned on before, having Coal's hand around mine teaching me how to pleasure him had my body growing wetter by the second. I brushed my finger along the head and found his most sensitive zones. This man's body was a work of art. Was he truly mine to enjoy for the rest of my hopefully very long life?

"My wolf. I can't keep holding him back." Sweat dotted Coal's brow, and his eyes were closed tight as though he were in pain.

"Stop fighting him, Coal. We are mates, I want you. All of you." I didn't even recognize the low, husky voice coming from my mouth. He wasn't the only one with a barely contained and impatient wolf.

With a guttural growl, Coal gave in. He released his hold on the beast, no longer fighting to maintain full control, and focused his calculating gaze on me.

I shivered at the feralness lurking in those glowing depths. But when he licked his lips, my fear dissipated, and my body threatened to spontaneously combust.

Face tightening, Coal parted my legs. These weren't just the eyes of a skilled predator... I was staring directly into the eyes of an alpha. Raw power hung heavy in the air around us.

This man could rule the world if it amused him. But Coal had chosen to live in a quiet part of the country and keep to himself. The werewolf community feared him based on the rumors, but they didn't have a clue of the true power of the Brimstone Alpha.

On instinct, I scooted away from the predator stalking me. Wrong move.

With a snarl, Coal's hands slid beneath my thighs. He held me still, preventing me from scooting away as he dropped his head and delved his tongue inside me.

"Coal!" I tried to scream his name, but it was little more than a hoarse cry.

The room spun as Coal's long tongue gave one unhurried stroke after another, his chest rumbling in approval as he tasted the evidence of my arousal. Part of me was embarrassed having his tongue in such an intimate place and wanted me to close my legs. But it was also incredibly erotic having this powerful man on his stomach in front of me, his tongue stirring sensations I hadn't in my wildest dreams thought possible.

My lust won, and I let my shoulders fall back against the bed. No longer trying to get away, I relaxed my legs and gave myself over to Coal. Moaning, I sank my fingers into his dark hair. Encouraged, Coal's mouth pressed harder against my core, and his tongue flicked faster, stirring my lust into a frenzy. By the time he pulled back, my legs were trembling, and my eyes refused to focus.

"Easy, Coal…" Aspen's voice warned from the shadows, shifting his body to move at a moment's notice.

Coal either didn't hear, or he was simply ignoring Aspen. Coal's hands wrapped around my waist, flipping me over. One minute I'd been on my back looking up at him, and the next, I was on my hands and knees, facing away from him with my body on display for him. The change of position had been fast and smooth, leaving me only enough time to gasp.

Gripping my hips slightly harder than necessary, Coal yanked my butt against his groin. I moaned at the scorching heat of his erection as he ground it against my aching core. Leaning down, his teeth grazed my shoulder. Coal's hot breath blew across the sensitive skin of my neck where I'd wear his mark after tonight.

Tilting my head to the side, I presented myself for his bite.

"Not yet," he growled, his teeth nipping at my skin.

Coal lined himself up with my slick heat. With one hard thrust, he buried himself deep, tearing the telltale sign that this was my first time. My vision darkened around the edges as pain tore through me.

"Freaking fruitcake!" I dropped onto my elbows and screamed into a fluffy pillow.

Coal held my hips, but he'd turned to stone. "Candi? This is your first time being with a man?"

"Yes," I hissed, breathing through the tiny aftershocks of pain.

The tightening of his fingers and harsh breathing were the only signs that he wasn't a statue. "Why didn't you tell me? I would have tried to be gentle."

I snorted. "Because I was a little embarrassed about it, and I didn't want you to be gentle. Plus, I've heard it's like a Band-Aid. Better to get it over quick."

The pain was all but gone, yet Coal remained motionless. My body began to quiver with the need for something more. I cautiously moved my hips, letting Coal's erection slide an inch. The delicious friction had me biting down on the pillow as pleasure threatened to drown me.

"Coal. Please. I need you." I hoped my begging would rouse him from his stupor.

A chair creaked as Frost shoved to his feet. "Seriously, Coal, if you aren't up for this, just say so and tap me in."

That seemed to snap the Brimstone Alpha out of his stupor. He snarled at Frost, daring him to take another step. "Mine."

Without giving me time to adjust, Coal pulled back and plunged inside me. My lungs forgot to work, and I struggled to breathe as he slid from me again. Harder and faster, he thrust himself into my silken heat until my body practically vibrated from the exquisite sensation.

Coal claimed my body with a hungry possessiveness that turned me on more than I'd ever admit out loud. My desire was rushing toward a crescendo.

"Coal! Coal!" I moaned his name while my heart pounded in my ears. With each stroke, the thing in my stomach tightened like a spring ready to uncoil. I wanted more, but I was more than a little terrified of what would happen when I came apart.

With a last hard thrust, Coal buried himself to the hilt.

Pleasure erupted inside me like a volcano. For a second, it was too much, and stars sparkled in my vision. My bones disappeared, turning my limbs to jelly.

I squeaked when Coal hauled me back, pressing my back flat against his chest. He buried himself inside me three more times before his teeth sank deep into my neck. His body stiffened, then shuddered, and I felt the heat of his release.

When Coal finished, he lowered me gently onto the cloud-soft comforter. Lying down beside me, he turned me in his arms to face him. His eyes had shifted back to the warm chocolate color that belonged to the human half of Coal.

I nuzzled his neck, drawing in a deep breath of his smoky scent before sinking my fangs into Coal's neck and marking him as mine. The Brimstone Alpha's hand shot to my throat. His fingers tightened around my neck for half a heartbeat, and I thought he was going to rip me away from him. Instead, he relaxed his grip, and his thumb stroked my skin. Claim staked, my wolf finally quieted.

"I've never heard of a female marking a male, but I am proud to bear my mate's mark." Coal sounded equal parts confused and amused. I tended to have that effect on people, so he'd eventually get used to it.

"And you never had a she-wolf come down your chimney before either, but here we are," I quipped playfully before scooting deeper under the blankets and snuggling into his chest. Coal's chest rumbled with laughter, and I smiled.

"You're mine, Coal," I whispered. My wolf and I were both wonderfully sated and already half asleep.

The bed dipped under Aspen and Frost's weight as they crawled into bed to cuddle me. I'd never felt so content. "You are all mine."

Chapter Nine

—CANDI—

With a yawn, I stretched like a cat, enjoying the soft fabric of the sheets brushing against my bare skin. Every part of my body was sore, but in the absolute best sort of way. I blinked in the hazy morning light that leaked through the dark floor-to-ceiling curtains, taking in the three sexy-as-cinnamon werewolves around me.

Coal was in front of me, his arm resting lightly over my waist. Frost sprawled sideways across the foot of the bed, his hand wrapped around my leg. Even though he hadn't marked me yet, the mate bond pushed him to keep some form of physical contact between us. Aspen snored softly behind me, his back snuggled tight against mine.

I'd never felt as comfortable or as loved as I did at that moment. Last night I'd run from my father to find my freedom, and I'd found something better… love.

"That's sweet. But it's too early to be awake, little mate," Coal grumbled, not bothering to open his eyes. "Go back to sleep."

My cheeks burned. I'd forgotten that once Coal marked me, a mental link would form between us. Well, this could be awkward.

"What did she say? It's not fair, we can't hear her yet!" Frost whined, propping himself onto his elbow to stare at me.

"Something about freedom, and she's falling in love with us. Now everyone shut up. This is why I keep you guys locked out of my room. No one should be up this early." Coal pulled a pillow over his head.

"You have the biggest bed, so I guess you won't be locking us out anymore." Frost smirked in Coal's direction, but gave me a mischievous wink.

"Aye. We love ye, lass." Aspen rolled over, nearly smothering me into a tight embrace.

Coal woke up in a hurry when my body was yanked away from him. Tossing the pillow aside, Coal's dark eyes pierced my very soul.

The mood shifted from playful to serious as Coal reached out and brushed his thumb along my bottom lip. "I love you so much it terrifies me."

I thought nothing scared Coal. If anything, he seemed like the type of man who enjoyed causing others to fear.

"I'm falling in love with you too, and I'm scared." I didn't bother trying to hide my raw fear. Letting them in was the hardest thing I'd ever done, but I wanted this more than I'd ever wanted something in my life. Trusting them was a risk I was willing to take.

A long howl echoed in the distance. Randolph. I jerked back against Aspen. My desperate escape from the previous night was still fresh in my mind, and it was making me jumpy.

Coal reached out and caught my chin in his hand. "Calm down, beautiful. They will never take you from us."

A second howl pierced the silence. The wolf was miles away, but the howl was much closer than the first. I shivered. The Evergreen pack was on its way.

Sighing and mumbling about only people who were possessed would be up this early, Coal rolled out of bed. My body warmed as I watched my magnificent mate dress. "The sooner we get this over with, the sooner they will be out of our lives."

Coal might be eager for the coming confrontation, but I certainly wasn't in the mood to deal with dear old dad. For the first time since my mother had passed away more than a decade ago, I'd woken up happy. And, of course, my father was coming to ruin it, just like he ruined every other part of my life. With that realization, I decided I was going to be petty as heck today.

Coal's lips curled into a wicked smile. "One day with Brimstone, and you're already releasing your dark side," he teased, having read my thoughts.

Grabbing a pillow, I tossed it at Coal's head. The infuriating man caught it deftly and launched it into Frost's unsuspecting face. Frost tumbled off the bed and hit the floor with a curse.

"Stop being lazy. If I have to be up at this horrible hour, you should be too. Besides, I want you as backup when our visitors arrive."

"Could I take a shower and brush my hair? I'd prefer to look put together, not like I just rolled out of bed. Would that be okay?" I gave Coal my best pleading eyes.

"I like the idea of you looking like you just rolled out of my bed and wearing my scent. But if you'll feel more comfortable, and it will give you pleasure to make them wait, then you should definitely take your time." Coal shrugged, seemingly unconcerned with how long I made a visiting alpha wait.

"The shower is through that door there." He motioned toward a door in the corner of the room. "You should find everything you need in there. I'll find you something to wear while you're showering."

Wiggling out of Aspen's hold, I turned and gave him a quick peck on the cheek before sliding out of bed. Frost smacked my butt as I rushed past him, earning him a scowl. I was too eager for a hot shower to deal with him, so I continued making my way to the bathroom.

Within minutes, I was in the shower. The hot spray felt incredible, massaging my sore muscles, and a quiet moan escaped my lips before I could stop it.

"Keep making those sexy little noises, and you'll be forced to share that shower," Frost's voice drifted through the closed door.

Reaching for the shampoo, I mumbled under my breath, "Freaking werewolf hearing."

"I have other werewolf abilities I think you might enjoy." Frost's deep laughter had my belly fluttering and my mind racing with mental images of him joining me in the shower.

"Frost! Downstairs with me. NOW!" Coal barked, and Frost groaned at the order.

You better watch those thoughts, sexy. Otherwise, you won't be leaving this bedroom at all today, Coal purred in my mind. *I doubt your father would appreciate being forced to wait outside in the cold while I ravish your body and make you scream.*

If his threat was meant to make me stop thinking about sliding down his 'northern pole,' he was sadly mistaken. The only thing that kept me from begging them to join me was the anxiety of knowing Evergreen wolves were on Coal's land.

Coal's voice softened in my mind. *It's your land too, Luna.*

I dropped the shampoo bottle. Luna? How had I forgotten about titles? I'd just wanted a place in Coal's pack... any place. Now I was his luna, and my father couldn't ever drag me back to Evergreen. Taking a luna was an act of war. It wasn't tolerated and was the one crime that would unite every werewolf pack on earth to a single cause... rescuing the kidnapped luna and making an example of the pack who dared take and house a stolen luna. I was safely out of my father's reach for the rest of my life.

No one will ever take you from us, Coal's voice whispered. *I know you need time to process everything, so I'm going to block out your thoughts now. If you want me, I'm here. Always.*

My salty tears mixed with the hot shower stream as a heavy weight rolled off my shoulders, and relief swelled inside me.

By the time I stepped out of the shower, I was ready to take on the day... and my father. I dried quickly and left the steam-filled bathroom with a towel wrapped around me.

Standing in the bedroom, I froze. What was I supposed to wear? The dirty clothes I'd worn last night were still downstairs, and I didn't fancy prancing around in a towel in front of the Evergreen pack. Fudge balls, I wasn't even sure I was ready to walk around in my birthday suit in front of my mates.

I nearly wept all over when I spotted the pair of gray jogging pants and a black shirt lying on the bed. The guys had already anticipated my needs and had tried their best to find me something clean to wear.

Slipping on the sweats that smelled of Frost, I tied them tight and rolled the band a couple of times to keep them up over my hips. The shirt was far too big, which was no surprise since the scent told me it belonged to Aspen. I twisted a quick knot in the front to give myself some semblance of a figure rather than one of a troll living under a bridge.

Glancing at my reflection in the mirror, I couldn't stop my grin. I looked happy. My eyes were bright, and my pale cheeks glowed. Long glossy blonde hair covered Coal's mate mark. I lifted my hand, intending to pull my hair back to show the mark to our guests, but thought better of it. It might be wiser to wait to see how the meeting played out first.

I made my way downstairs to find Coal, Frost, and Aspen sitting relaxed on an oversized dark leather couch. Directly across from my mates sat the Evergreen Beta, who was glaring daggers at me... and my father.

My heart stuttered, and I nearly missed my footing on the stairs when my eyes landed on the werewolf Elder sitting quietly in a chair by the window.

It was rare for an alpha to call on an Elder, and even rarer for an Elder to travel in person to handle a dispute. Usually, the Elders required all parties to come to them. The fact that my father had actually called in an Elder showed how desperate he was to get me back. But why? Would he go this far just over his hurt pride?

The Elder's head turned toward me, and his lips parted in a smile.

My hand shook on the polished banister as I moved down the last two steps. I guess we were about to find out.

Chapter Ten

—CANDI—

"**T**here she is now," Coal spoke with cold formality, his expression bored. "Darling, we have company." A pang of sadness shot through me, and I fought the urge to drag Coal back to the bedroom, desperate to see the warmth return to his eyes.

Reaching out, Coal caught my hand and pulled me down onto his lap. His arms snaked around my waist, tucking my body into his chest. Coal rested his chin on my shoulder and took a deep breath, drawing my scent into his lungs and not bothering to hide it.

The PDA, a.k.a. public display of affection, from the Brimstone Alpha, was unexpected... but oh, so welcome. Turning my face, I nuzzled my cheek against his before relaxing into him. I sighed in contentment, my mate's reassuring touch quickly banishing my anxiety.

"Really, Candi? What has gotten into you? You've never displayed such a blatant show of disrespect as you are exhibiting right now." My father's words carried the sting of his disapproval.

"And who are you to be speaking to her like that?" Aspen demanded, leaning forward with fire crackling in his eyes.

It was that very moment when I realized I'd forgotten to tell the men one very important detail.

I'd never told them who my father was.

"Um, guys—" I began, but was cut off by my father.

"I'm her father, and I'll talk to her however I please." He sneered at Aspen.

All three of my mates stared at me, their eyes widening a fraction.

"Surprise?" I squeaked.

Frost looked amused. Aspen seemed confused. Coal's face lost all expression, giving away nothing of what he was thinking or feeling. I'd hoped Coal might have picked up the familial connection through our new mind link, but I guess he hadn't caught that juicy tidbit. What if he thought I'd tricked him into biting me? Would he hate me after this? He probably regretted marking me.

I don't regret marking you. My only regret is I have to entertain guests instead of spending the day in bed with you. We'll talk about this later, Coal tried to calm me through the mind link.

I didn't get to respond because Randolph lurched off the couch. "Candi, this is unacceptable. I will not be forced to

88

sit here and watch you make out with a male wolf just to get a rise out of me. Come sit over here until we are ready to leave, and I might forgive you for this." He pointed to the cushion next to him as though I were a naughty puppy who needed to be shown where to sit.

"No, Randolph. I'm going to stay right here." It felt unbelievably good to say the word 'no' to Randolph.

I'd survived years of him ignoring me, then bullying me, and lately, treating me like he owned me. The entire time, my father ignored it all and continued to tell me what a perfect match Randolph was for me.

I sat up a little straighter. Never again would I be made to feel less than by either of the men in front of me.

That's my girl, Coal praised through the link. *You're a treasure, and they were too stupid to realize it.*

Randolph's face turned an ugly shade of crimson, and he opened his mouth, but before he could speak, the Elder tapped his cane on the floor. Everyone's attention turned to the older wolf.

"Regarding the matter at hand." The Elder cleared his throat. "By law, the Evergreen pack does have the right to take Candi home. They came to retrieve her within hours of her trespassing on Brimstone territory."

The Evergreen wolves smirked while my mates rumbled a protest.

Ignoring the men's reactions, the Elder continued. "Alpha Coal, you granted her mercy and did not execute her. However, that does not automatically give you the

89

right to keep her here, especially when her pack has expressly stated their wish to have her returned."

"What about what I want? Do you know how I ended up here?" I asked, frustrated that the Elders would condone my father's archaic method of pairing me with a mate.

The Elder shot my father a glare of disgust. "Yes, I'm aware of the situation." He turned to me, studying my face closely.

"There are many old laws in sore need of changing. Maybe someday there will be an alpha ready to challenge these unfair laws. Sadly, I must make my judgments based on the laws as they're written. You're to be returned to your father and pack." The Elder's face held pity and sadness. "My hands are tied."

It was time to play my ace. I tilted up my chin in defiance. "I will not leave my mates."

"Aye, she won't be leaving us," Aspen added.

Coal's arms tightened imperceptibly around me, and a muscle in his jaw ticked.

"Your what?" my father roared in outrage, springing to his feet. "You better not have let one of these Brimstone wolves put his filthy mark on your neck!"

My father's face shifted from blood red to a purplish eggplant color, and the veins in his neck protruded. He'd never shown me affection, so this seemed like a complete overreaction. I knew he hated his little game being messed up, but shouldn't he have been relieved that I was no longer his problem?

Coal stood, pulling me up with him and cradling me

tighter to him. Aspen and Frost moved in a blur to stand in front of us, mostly blocking my view of the enraged Evergreen Alpha. I loved how my mates wanted to protect me, but it was time for me to stand up for myself.

I'd been scared when I ran, but underneath that fear had been the faint pulsing of power. At first, I'd thought it was from taking back control of my life and my freedom, but it'd been growing steadily stronger. This was a battle I needed to fight for myself.

Extricating myself from Coal's hold, I moved between Frost and Aspen. I stepped forward, stopping when I was toe-to-toe with my ex-alpha. He was taller than me by two feet, but I didn't care. I was done being intimidated by him.

"Lower your voice. I will not allow you to speak to me this way." My voice vibrated with command.

My father's eyes widened with shock and, to my shock, he went utterly silent. I hadn't actually expected that to work. Perhaps my defiance had stunned him to the point of being speechless?

Taking advantage of his silence, I continued. "Alpha Coal, Frost, and Aspen are my soulmates."

"Lies!" my father tried to shout, but the word was nothing more than a hoarse whisper.

The Elder's chair scraped the hardwood as he pushed to his feet. "Do you have proof they are your soulmates?"

Locking eyes with my father, I pulled my hair back into a ponytail. Coal's bite was clearly visible, proof that I'd not only found my soulmates, but that I was claimed.

"Interesting," the Elder hummed softly. Moving closer,

he took his time studying the mark on my neck. Straightening, he turned to my father and spoke in a neutral tone. "Alpha Coal is her mate. You no longer have any claim on your daughter. She's free to stay with Alpha Coal's pack for as long as she so chooses."

My father's face morphed into a mask of horror.

"What kind of sick joke is this? There has to be a way to undo it!" Randolph turned on my father, rage twisting his features. "You promised all I had to do was convince Candi to be my mate before she turned twenty-five, and you would make me the next alpha!"

"This is your fault! If you had just done what you were supposed to and wooed the dense girl, then I wouldn't have had to call a mate hunt!"

My stomach turned to lead, and bile rose in my throat. They had realized I would never accept Randolph as my mate, and came up with a plan to force me into becoming his mate. The mate hunt had been a setup.

Randolph's desire to claim me had nothing to do with him actually wanting me as his mate. His sudden change from being my bully to fake kindness had been solely to lure me into a bond with him. Deep down, I'd known, but the confirmation left a sour taste in my mouth.

My vision blurred with tears at the realization of how close I'd come to a loveless mating.

Coal's arms tightened around me, silently reassuring me I wasn't alone and that could never happen now.

The Elder turned to me, a brilliant smile on his lips.

"There is another old law, and I think you might actually like this one, little lady."

My father paled and stepped forward. "No, this doesn't —" The Elder lifted his cane and jabbed my father in the chest.

"Alpha Evergreen, I suggest you don't interrupt me." The Elder refocused on me and continued. "Your mother was the only child of Evergreen's previous alpha and luna. She married your father, and several years later, they had you. When she tragically passed, your father continued to lead the Evergreen pack as alpha."

The Elder's face was animated, and his brows rose as though he was waiting for us to catch some hidden meaning or punchline. "Your father led as alpha, even though he had no blood claim to the title."

When no one spoke or reacted, the Elder pinched the bridge of his nose as though his patience was running out. "Werewolf law requires that all alphas must be from alpha bloodlines, but it does have a provision for extremely rare cases such as this. Since your grandparents and mother were deceased, and you were far too young to lead, your father could lead as alpha in your place. The law is very clear that when you claim a mate, or when you turn twenty-five, the Evergreen pack becomes yours."

Reality slammed into me like a runaway freight train. I turned twenty-five next week. By werewolf law, I would've been handed the reins to lead my pack since I was the one who carried the alpha bloodline... not through my father, but through my mother.

My father would've been forced to step down. Something he'd never do willingly. He'd purposefully kept this information from me. The room's temperature spiked as my fury burned out of control.

He'd tried to force me into a relationship with Randolph because he could control the younger male wolf and maintain his position of power over Evergreen. My father probably viewed Randolph's willingness to bully me into submission as a sign he could keep me under control. I was nothing more than a pawn to my father in his quest for power.

The Elder stepped in front of me, unable to hide his triumphant grin. "Congrats on your mating, and congrats on your new pack, Alpha Candi. I know you and your mates will do wonderful things for Evergreen."

Holy Holly! This had to be a joke. I had been so focused on my father's betrayal, I hadn't even realized what this meant for my mates and me. How were we going to run Brimstone and Evergreen? In a wide-eyed panic, I spun around to face my mates.

Frost looked positively giddy.

Aspen's chest was puffed out in pride.

Coal? Well, he looked like he had seen a ghost. The ghost of Christmas, perhaps?

His reaction distracted me from my meltdown, and I grinned in wicked delight at the thought of how much fun I was going to have dragging my Scrooge of a mate through Evergreen's holiday festivities.

Clearly having read my thoughts, his horrified eyes turned to me.

For the first time since my mother passed away, I found myself looking forward to Christmas in Evergreen.

Chapter Eleven

—FROST—

"This is insane! Do you even hear what you're saying?" the Evergreen Alpha shouted, spit flying from his mouth. How could sweet Candi come from this vile wolf? "A female can't be an alpha! It's unnatural and unheard of."

I bristled even if the Elder remained unruffled as he spoke. "I suggest you remember who you are speaking to, Kristof."

If I hadn't been working to control my own fury, and my wolf's incessant demand to drag our little mate to safety, I might have laughed at the ex-alpha's horror over being called by his first name. It was worse than if the Elder had actually slapped him in the face.

Candi's poker face was nonexistent. Every emotion she was feeling tumbled across her expressive features. My heart ached for her, and I had to dig my nails into my palms to keep from grabbing her and making a run for it. Anything to get her away from here.

Is she okay? I asked Coal.

Coal shot me a disgusted look. *Of course not. She's on a runaway emotional rollercoaster right now. It's a wonder she hasn't broken down yet,* he snarled in my mind. *If she didn't want to stand on her own right now, Kristof would be ten feet under already.*

I swallowed my jealousy that Coal had a mind link with her, and I didn't. Not yet, anyway. While male wolves within a pack could speak to each other through a mental link, the female wolves were only able to speak to their mate telepathically. There were various theories as to why this might be.

Two of the worst, but sadly most popular theories were the demeaning idea that female wolves lacked the mental strength to deal with a mental pack bond, and the misogynistic idea that a link between a female and her mate helped to ensure she was reliant on him to communicate on her behalf.

I personally thought the most likely explanation was probably due to male werewolves' lack of self-control and extreme neediness. We'd probably lose our minds if an unmated male wolf spoke to our mate through the mental link. Let's face it, we were jealous and emotionally unstable when it came to our mates.

You may be right. The Elders have spent many a night pondering this, and we believe it might be nature's way of trying to ensure our species multiplies. Wolves are social, and isolating female wolves from a mental bond with their pack mates, could push she-wolves into craving a connection to another wolf, which would lead to mating and reproducing. Nature can be cruel sometimes, the Elder spoke in my mind, shaking his head sadly.

My gaze landed on Randolph and Kristof. I hated men like them. Males who would never see a she-wolf as their equal.

My mind was spinning, trying to think back over all my werewolf history lessons. Hard as I tried, I couldn't think of a single female alpha. Kristof might be right. Maybe the Elder was mistaken, and females couldn't be an alpha. I cringed at the thought. If anyone deserved to be an alpha, it was Candi.

"I'm not mistaken, pup." The Elder pinned me with narrowed eyes and spoke out loud.

Pup? I hadn't been considered a pup for several decades. And why was he still reading my thoughts?

The Elder snorted and again answered aloud. "When you are my age, anyone under a hundred is a pup. To answer your unspoken question, I'm reading everyone's thoughts. This drama is better than a Telenovela."

I shrugged. If I had the Elders' ability to read everyone's mind, I'd probably do the same.

Banging his cane on the ground, the Elder addressed everyone in the room. "Candi is Evergreen pack's new alpha. This isn't open to negotiation. There have been a few female alphas over the centuries, and they were incredible leaders. Sadly, our society has forgotten their stories. Likely on purpose."

He narrowed his eyes on Kristof.

"I refuse to bow down to a female! I'll die before subjecting myself to being humiliated like that," Randolph stated, his lip curling.

"Your death can easily be arranged." Aspen cracked his knuckles. "Are ye busy right now?"

Kristof rested a hand on Randolph's shoulder. "That won't be necessary. Once Candi is your mate, you will lead Evergreen as the alpha."

"Candi bears my mark. She won't be mating with Randolph." Coal's chest rumbled with a warning growl.

"I'm not blind. Your mark is quite visible on my daughter's neck." Kristof emphasized the word *daughter*, giving a sad smile as though he'd been hurt by not being included in her decision. "But I noticed Candi stated all three of you were her mates. I'll admit, I was scandalized by the idea, but now it makes sense. Candi can also mate with Randolph, an Evergreen male. Alpha Coal is far too busy with Brimstone to worry over tiny little Evergreen, anyway. Randolph is far more familiar with Evergreen and can lead it as alpha once he mates with Candi."

When he finished speaking, Kristof looked around the room as though he expected us to be wowed by his brilliant idea. I wondered which of us could rip his head off the fastest. Probably Aspen. He was like a freaking sasquatch and inching closer to them by the second.

Candi's mouth fell open, and she stared at Kristof. "Is your butthole jealous of all the crap that just came out of your mouth?"

I guffawed loud enough to scare away every bird within a mile radius. Coal's stone mask cracked just a bit, and the edge of his mouth tipped up in a smile. Aspen hid his grin behind his beefy hand. Our little Candi Cane has some spice!

"I can't believe you are still trying to steal away my birthright. Evergreen is mine, and I intend to lead my wolves MYSELF. Evergreen deserves an alpha who cares more about the pack than their ego." Candi took a step toward her father, fire burning in her eyes. "And I will never accept Randolph as my mate. Fate gave me three mates, and Randolph wasn't one of them."

Blind rage ripped away the calm mask Kristof had been wearing. "If you lack morals and are willing to open your legs to three male wolves, why shouldn't you take another? These three must get off on sharing, so they shouldn't have a problem watching you ride a fourth male. The more the merrier, right?"

The words had been directed at Candi, but they still knocked the wind out of my lungs. How could he talk about his daughter like that? Kristof had gone too far. My shock turned to an inferno of hatred so deep I worried I might never escape it. As one, Coal, Aspen, and I lunged for the disgusting ex-alpha. Once we ripped out his throat, he'd never be able to disrespect our mate again.

"Stop! No one move!" Candi's shout echoed off the walls.

The words slammed into my gut like a physical punch. My body was already obeying the alpha order before my mind had even registered it. Alpha commands didn't work on me as I was an alpha, so why had my wolf followed the order like I was an omega?

I tried to turn my head, but my body refused to move. Giving up, I slid my eyes toward the Elder, expecting him to have given the command. To my utter disbelief, he stood wide-eyed and frozen like the rest of us. Only one person in the room was moving... Candi.

Did she just give an alpha order? I hissed into Coal's mind, still struggling to accept the obvious.

Coal's brow wrinkled in confusion. *Yes, she did.*

But how? Alpha commands aren't supposed to work on us, and they sure as Hades aren't supposed to work on any Elders, Aspen growled into the link.

I don't know how, Coal snapped. *But I don't think this is the first time she used it. Yesterday, she told me to stop when I was carrying her upstairs, and I obeyed.*

You're right. She used it on the porch too, I murmured, stunned we hadn't noticed what had been right under our noses. A freaking female alpha.

Candi's chest heaved, and I caught the slight tremor in her hand. Alpha energy so pure radiated through her until she seemed to glow like the star on a Christmas tree.

I tried to open my mouth and speak, but my jaw remained locked. When she said *don't move,* she meant it. Allowing the full weight of my alpha power to fill me, I pushed against Candi's hold. It was useless.

Can you break free, Coal? As acting Alpha of Brimstone, he was the most powerful of the three of us.

No. I can't even get the command to so much as crack. She's holding us in place, and we are stuck until she decides to release us. Even inside the mental link, I could practically feel Coal's pride.

I was proud too, but I'd be a lot happier if I could blink my eyes, or better yet, throat-punch Randolph.

Candi had been motionless while thinking through her next move. Taking a deep breath, she walked toward Randolph, raw power crackling along her skin. "On your knees."

My mate didn't shout the command. She didn't need to. Her power slammed into the Evergreen Beta like a runaway Zamboni. Randolph dropped to his knees at her feet. His body had obeyed her order, but the fury in his eyes and tightening of his jaw showed his defiance. It didn't go unnoticed by Candi.

"You may speak, but I suggest you think carefully about what you choose to say next." Candi's brow rose as she waited for the man before her to speak.

Randolph wasted no time. "Just because you are a freak of nature who can force me to kneel doesn't mean I will ever recognize you as my alpha."

I didn't have to be a psychic to see Randolph's future. He was about to take a trip to hell on a sleigh covered in adorable jingle bells.

Chapter Twelve

—CANDI—

Time seemed to slow as I looked into Randolph's hate-filled eyes. Memories flashed through my mind, images of every time he went out of his way to make sure I cried myself to sleep. When we were younger, it had been small things like dumping my lunch on the ground or pulling my long braid.

With each passing year it had escalated, the name-calling grew more creative, the acts so much worse, and by the time we were teenagers, his constant bullying had destroyed my self-worth and confidence, leaving me in a constant state of looking over my shoulder.

Randolph didn't even have to get his hands dirty while tormenting me in high school because he had his own little posse who were eager to score points with him by any means necessary. How many classes had I missed because

I'd been locked in a closet or the bathroom? How many times had my homework been yanked from my hand and destroyed minutes before it was due? How many bruises had covered my body from being body-checked every time he passed me in the halls? Too many to count.

Some of the memories I'd managed to bury; almost forgotten. But others kept me up crying on sleepless nights. Like Freshman year, when I'd cried into the dirt while Randolph shaved off every strand of my long blonde hair while his friends cheered encouragement. I'd worn a hoodie for months as my hair grew back in.

Another painful memory was my senior prom night. I'd made friends with a low-ranking male wolf. He was safe. Even if he was awkward, he was nice and asked me to go with him. It would have been my first date, and I'd spent hours daydreaming about it. My father hadn't seen the point in spending money on useless clothing, so I'd gotten a job at the coffee shop and saved every penny to buy my dream dress and matching shoes.

When I'd gone to get ready for the dance, I'd found my beautiful deep violet dress lying in ribbons on the floor of my room. My bedroom window was open, and a note had been taped to the glass. Through my tears, I'd recognized Randolph's handwriting.

If you are so eager for another guy to touch you, go naked and see what happens. For now, I'm enjoying screwing with your mind, but soon I will enjoy screwing you so hard, you won't be able to walk. From your thoughts to your body, you're mine.

Don't try this again, or I will be ripping the dress from your body instead of from the hanger.

I sank to my bedroom floor and sobbed until there were no tears left in my body. My father had been too caught up in his own affairs to bother checking on me, and so I'd fallen asleep on the floor surrounded by the shredded purple silk remnants of my destroyed dress.

The following morning, I'd taken what was left of my silk gown and the crumpled note to my father's office. Even though he had always turned a blind eye to the treatment his own daughter had received at the hand of the pack, I'd believed that this time, he would step in... that he would act like a real dad who worried about his little girl.

Instead, my father chuckled as he read the note, mumbling something about the boy knowing what he wanted. He tried to convince me it was normal behavior for a young male wolf in love, and that my having a date had just spurred Randolph into realizing how much I meant to him. My father had tried to convince me this twisted kind of love was *normal*, and that I should be happy for Randolph's attention and not seriously concerned for my safety.

It was clear my dad was pleased with the idea of a match between Randolph and me, and it didn't matter how much pain Randolph had caused me, my dad was choosing the son he wanted over me. That morning had been a hard-to-swallow dose of reality check, but I finally accepted I was truly alone in the world. Not a single soul cared about me.

The people in my life only cared about how I could benefit or amuse them.

That was when something inside of me died. I'd left my father's office, dried my tears, and locked my emotions away. Better to feel nothing at all than to only feel pain. But as I threw away the tattered violet fabric, I determined that if I could control nothing else in my life, I was going to ensure I would never become Randolph's mate, or let myself believe that his cruelty was simply a misguided attempt to show me love. If that was love, I didn't want it.

Little mate, release me, Coal's pain-filled words brushed my mind. *Stop pushing me out of your mind. Let me in. Let me take care of you.*

Shaking my head to clear it of the fog from my past, I hadn't even realized I'd been blocking him, at least partially, from the mental link. My gut twisted. How much had he heard?

I want to hear it all, Coal answered in my mind. *But I definitely heard enough to know these men must die.*

I lifted my fingertips to my neck and brushed them along the raised skin of Coal's mark. In twelve hours, the grinch of the werewolf species had shown me more kindness and love than my pack and father had shown me in over twelve years. All three of my guys had.

It would take a while for my internal scars to heal, but I never had to feel powerless again. I studied the face of the man I'd called father, and the jerk who thought he was prince charming. They'd messed with the wrong alpha, and I wanted them to pay for the past and present.

I began to hum. *Chestnuts roasting on an open fire.*

Except, in this case, I was the fire, and I was ready to start cracking some Christmas nuts.

Laughter rumbled in my mind, and it wasn't Coal's or my own. Great, I'd finally lost it.

Candi, would you mind releasing me from the command? I'm afraid these old bones aren't as spry as they used to be, and I'm getting a little stiff. They call me an Elder for a reason. The voice drifted into my mind.

Heart lurching into my throat, I spun to face the Elder, having completely forgotten he was in the room. When I'd given the alpha command, I wasn't entirely sure what I had been doing, but it definitely hadn't been intended as an order for him. I'd just wanted to stop the bloodshed before it began and give myself a moment to think. Why had my order worked on an Elder? I winced. He was probably going to be ticked off at my disrespect.

"You are free to…" I hesitated. Why did this feel like a really weird version of Simon Says? "To sit down and get comfortable?" My voice rose at the end, making it more of a question than a statement.

Released from my order, the Elder stretched his back and gave me a smile. "Stop worrying. I'm not angry. I'm intrigued by this new development."

The Elder studied the two Evergreen males, shaking his head in disgust. "I know you want your revenge, and you are very much entitled to it, but I think it's best if I escort your father and Randolph back to Evergreen before things get messy and legal factors come into play. We've already intruded enough on your first morning as a mated wolf, and if the thoughts running through Aspen and Frost's minds are any indication, you are going to have a long day." The Elder smirked at the blush warming my cheeks.

Peeking over my shoulder at my three mates, I sucked in a breath at the hunger glinting in their eyes.

To my shock, my father didn't argue with the Elder. He blew out a long sigh and dropped his head in defeat. "The Elder is right. I can see how you feel about Randolph, Candi. And I have no desire to go against a ruling from the Elders. It's best I return to Evergreen and start moving my things out of the way. This is going to be a weird transition for both of us." Kristof grabbed Randolph's shoulder and yanked him off the floor.

"Are you serious? You're just going to give up?" Randolph spluttered, struggling to break free of Kristof's hold.

"Enough!" Kristof snapped. "Show the Elder some respect."

I turned to the Elder and opened my mouth, but he answered my question before I'd even asked. "Yes, I will be there when you arrive to take over full control of the pack. We will expect you in two days."

Pushing the two Evergreen men out the front door, the Elder glanced back at me and spoke in my mind. *Thank you for showing mercy, Alpha Candi, and giving Kristof two days to move his things from the alpha's house. It was an undeserved kindness. I will make good use of this time as well. I want to speak*

with the other Elders to see if they know how it's possible for you
to have multiple mates, and how you left that mark on Coal's
neck. I've never heard of a female claiming a male. Very odd. I
hope to have answers for you when we meet next.

There was no hiding my snort. Odd was the understate-
ment of the year. I hadn't realized the Elder had noticed the
mark on Coal's neck, though. He certainly didn't miss
much.

"Randolph." The word rumbled from Coal's chest like
thunder.

The Evergreen Beta shot Coal a nasty look. "Yes?"

"You should have died for your treatment of Candi.
Against my better judgment, you are being allowed to leave
Brimstone land still breathing. But if you ever touch my
luna again, you will die. My respect for the Elder will not
stop me from feeding your body to the vultures."

Randolph's face twisted, and his body began to shift.

"Enough. Out!" the Elder barked, shoving Randolph
onto the porch.

The door closed with a thud, and I stood staring at it,
my hands clenched at my sides. I wasn't sure if I was
relieved or angry that the Elder had whisked Kristof and
Randolph away before I gave into my pain and made them
hurt too.

Arms slid around my waist, tugging me against a warm
chest. Tilting my head back, I met Frost's icy blue eyes.

"Are you okay?" Frost leaned down to kiss my forehead.

My heart melted at his concern for me. Instead of

answering, I turned around in his arms and, going up on my tiptoes, I pressed my lips to his.

As long as I had these incredible men in my life, I was more than okay.

Chapter Thirteen
—ASPEN—

I 'd forced myself to sit, or I was going to hunt—and hurt—a beta. My fingers dug into the arms of the chair as the door shut behind our unwanted guests. The urge to shift into my wolf and go after them was like a siren's call in my mind, tempting me to forget rules and do what I was made to do: protect and destroy.

Alpha blood flowed through my veins, but I didn't want to lead. No, I enjoyed being an enforcer, the one to hand out judgment when an order was disobeyed. And right now, I wanted to rip Kristof's legs from his body and shove them up his arrogant arse for the way he'd dare speak to my mate.

I'd never been a fan of the Evergreen's ex-Alpha, but it was Randolph who really excited my bloodlust. I didn't know the details of what had happened between them, but clearly, something had. I'd seen the hurt in Candi's eyes, and I hadn't missed the way his howl caused her to flinch in my arms this morning. He didn't deserve to be in the room with my sweet little mate, and yet he felt entitled to her body and her position as alpha. My muscles tensed. I only needed one good reason to treat him like my personal piñata, and he'd given me several.

I restrained myself. Barely. The Elder and Candi had come to an agreement, and I wouldn't go against what my mate wanted. But the minute she gave so much as a nod of approval, I was going to push Coal out of the way to be the first to release my fangs and rip out both men's necks.

Closing my eyes, I took slow deep breaths through my nose and worked to recall my bloodlust. It wasn't an easy task to shove my instincts as an enforcer back into submission once it was awakened. It took several minutes of filling my nose with my mate's scent to calm down, but when I opened my eyes, my thirst for blood had quieted to a dull itch instead of an all-consuming demand. It was the lust part of the bloodlust that was still an issue.

My body hummed with my wolf's power—power I was supposed to be using on handing out one-way trips to Hades. I'd been denied the joy of ripping out the throats of those poor excuses for men, and now my body needed a way to release the raw energy. To make matters worse, the room stank of werewolf testosterone from the confrontation. Each deep breath brought the scent deeper into my lungs and left its acrid taste coating my tongue. It was the werewolf equivalent of waving a red cape in front of an angry bull.

These men had wanted to take my mate. The mate I hadn't even claimed yet. Their scent was in my home, reminding me of the threat they posed.

MINE.

I wasn't sure if it was my wolf or myself who'd spoken the word in my mind. Maybe it was both of us.

Frost's voice pulled me from the internal whirlpool of chaos threatening to drown me.

"Come on, Candi. Let's get you something to eat. It's been a long day, and it isn't even noon." He reluctantly released her from his embrace and caught her hand as he pulled her toward the kitchen.

Coal watched them leave the room and pinched the bridge of his nose. "I hate it, but I need to take care of some pack business that doesn't involve going after the Evergreen pack."

"Can't it wait?" It was difficult to speak through the strain on my body.

How could he leave her only hours after claiming her? Most newly claimed wolves don't leave their room for a week.

"If it could wait, I wouldn't leave her. This needs to be taken care of before she goes back to Evergreen to meet the Elder," Coal snarled, barely restraining his wolf.

I nodded. Coal was an incredible alpha. If he said it was important, then it was important.

Coal paused at the front door and pinned me with glowing eyes. "Don't hurt her, Aspen."

Not sure what he meant, I raised my eyebrow and waited for clarification.

"I'm not an idiot." Coal's fangs flashed, and he gave a harsh laugh. "Right now, you're fighting a losing battle. Your wolf will win, and you will be balls deep in our little mate before I return. Aspen, don't forget how freaking huge you are. You've been my friend since we were pups, but if you hurt her, I'll kill you."

"I'd never hurt my mate." I ground the words out, furious Coal would suggest I'd hurt Candi.

"OUR mate. I'm barely keeping it together. It's one thing to agree to share her, it's another to know that another man will be touching her in ways I want to be touching her. Don't test me." Coal had switched from friend to Brimstone Alpha in the blink of an eye. Blowing out a harsh breath, he spoke a bit calmer. "I've spent the morning in and out of her mind. She wants you, Aspen. Candi needs to know she is loved and belongs somewhere. Get your crap together and claim her."

Coal didn't wait for a response. The front door clicked closed behind him, leaving me alone to fight against the need battering against my self-control like a hurricane. Candi's soft laughter drifted from the kitchen, and I clenched my fists and fought the urge to rush to her side. As much as I hated to admit it, Coal was right.

Size-wise, Candi and I weren't exactly an ideal match. No matter how gentle I was, mating with me was going to cause her some discomfort. If I took her now, with the cocktail of lust, anger, and alpha energy swirling in my body, I'd likely explode and lose it. I was under more pressure than a shaken soda, and I didn't want to hurt her.

What if I took her how my wolf wanted, and she hated me later? Worse, what if the trust in her sweet eyes turned to fear?

The murmur of Frost's voice, followed by Candi's lilting tone, sent a sharp spike of jealousy piercing my chest. Maybe if I sat at the table and watched her eat, it would calm my agitated wolf. I was striding toward the kitchen before I'd finished the thought.

I realized my mistake the moment Candi came into view. Frost was busy emptying the contents of the well-stocked refrigerator onto the island in the middle of the kitchen.

"Seriously, Frost, anything is fine. I'm not picky!" Candi faced away from me, so she hadn't noticed me yet.

What I saw was Candi leaning forward on the island in an effort to see all the food options spread across the granite counter. What my wolf saw was Candi's adorable little butt being presented to us. An image of her spread out on the island burned into my brain, and I dropped my hand to adjust a certain part of my anatomy that had grown painfully hard.

Take her. My wolf was salivating over his mate's body.

The dangerous energy flowing through my veins began to spark from my skin. I was a powder keg with a lit fuse, and I needed to get out of the house and release some of the power before I became a human firecracker.

Taking a step back, I winced when the floorboard creaked, giving away my presence.

Candi spun around, her eyes lighting up when they landed on me. "Aspen! Where are you going?"

I took another step back until she spoke again.

What she said was, "Come here and eat with me."

What I heard was, "Come here and eat me."

Who was I to deny her? Especially when she asked so sweetly.

I blurred across the room toward her.

Frost shut the refrigerator door just in time to see my eyes shift from human to predator. His skin paled, and my wolf smirked. He knew he couldn't stop me. No one could. Frost was a powerful male, but my abnormally large body was unusual among werewolves. It was strange to know that even among werewolves, I stood out as a monster.

"ASPEN!" Frost threw himself in front of Candi. "RUN, Candi! Get out of here!"

Idiot. My wolf rolled his eyes over Frost's futile attempt to prevent me from getting to my mate.

I tossed him out of the way. If it had been any other wolf besides Frost or Coal, I would have killed him.

I slid my left arm across the countertop, knocking the various vegetables, fruits, eggs, and sauce jars to the floor with a horrific crash. Circling my right arm around Candi's waist, I tossed her onto the counter. She sat facing me, her legs drawn up in front of her as though she might scramble backward.

"If you don't want this. You need to give me an alpha

order." My eyes flickered between those of a human and my wolf. "You can't outrun me, and it would take an entire pack of wolves to pull me off you."

Her breath was coming in quick gasps, and my heart sank. She was scared of me.

Had my wolf been human, he would have smacked his head. *Not scared. She's excited. Smell her?*

Grabbing her ankles, I yanked her toward me and pressed my face against the crotch of her pants. I inhaled the molasses-sweet scent of her arousal, and my mouth went dry.

"Order me to stop. Before I hurt you." My canines had lengthened, causing my speech to be garbled, or maybe it was muffled because my face was still buried between her legs, unable to get enough of my mate's pheromones.

"Do it, Candi! He's about to snap!" Frost's voice came from somewhere behind me, but I ignored him.

Candi pressed her hands to either side of my face, and I allowed her to lift my head up. "Please," she whimpered, and my heart dropped until she said, "take me."

I stopped fighting against my nature and trusted that the moon goddess knew what she was doing when she paired Candi with me.

Sliding my thumbs into the waistband of her sweat-pants, I yanked them off in a single smooth motion. Candi didn't have time to react before I'd hauled her hips off the counter and brought her dripping heat to my mouth. She gasped as her back slammed against the cool granite, and then gasped a second time when my tongue plunged deep inside her.

I continued to lift her hips to give myself better access until only her shoulders and upper back rested against the counter, and her legs were wrapped around my head. She was making little mewling sounds, but I was too far gone to know if they were sounds of pleasure or pain. She had the power to stop me if I went too far.

Licking up every drop of her nectar, I growled in frustration when some of it evaded me, too deep for my tongue. That was easily fixed, and Candi moaned when my tongue pushed deeper. I renewed my efforts, twisting and curling my tongue inside her tight walls as I tried to drink my little mate dry.

Candi panted and squirmed, her legs clamping around my head like a vice. Not willing to risk my prize getting away, my fingers dug into the skin of her hips, holding her still. Pressing my mouth harder against her entrance, I gave a deep rumbling growl that sent vibrations through her body. She screamed as she climaxed, and her velvet walls clamped around my tongue.

My reward was a fresh wave of her slick arousal coating my tongue. I growled in encouragement and was surprised when a second orgasm ripped through her. Candi screamed my name and shuddered against my mouth. I could have tasted her all day, but my erection had swelled to the point it was painful, and my jeans felt like sandpaper.

Mate. Claim. Mate. Claim.

The demand repeated in my mind.

I released her hips, letting Candi's body drop down on the counter. She lay still, trying to catch her breath.

I shoved my pants down over my hips, sighing in relief as my erection sprang free. Before my pants even hit the floor around my ankles, I circled a hand around my heavy girth. With my other hand, I grabbed Candi's waist and slid her across the counter, impaling her on my length with a single hard thrust. She felt amazing.

Candi screamed, and her nails dug into my skin. This only further incited the beast and, gripping her hips, I pulled out and slammed back inside her. The sharp slap of skin on skin as I drove myself into her, forcing her tight channel to stretch and accept my full length, was music to my ears.

"Aspen. Aspen!" Candi's cry seemed to be a thousand miles away, calling to the human part of me.

I couldn't have answered if I'd wanted to. I was a werewolf with a bone—*boner?* Nothing was going to pull me from my lust-induced trance. Candi screamed, and her body clamped down on my erection as she rode out the waves of pleasure from her third orgasm. My beast held out, though, determined to ensure she had nothing more to give before giving in to my own release.

With her body attempting to strangle my length, my own release built despite my efforts not to—magma waiting to explode. Snarling, I grabbed her waist and spun her so that she faced away from me with her stomach pressing against the counter. I pinned her hips against the counter and curled my fingers over her hip bones to protect them from being bruised against the granite.

My thrusts were hard and rough, bordering on vicious; a beast claiming my mate and showing her the depth of the raw need she stirred in me. There was a primal urge to prove to my mate that I was capable of satisfying her. Over and over.

"Oh! Aspen." Candi's breathing was harsh.

Was she satisfied? In pain? I was too far gone to understand the nuances of human behavior. Thankfully, I did understand what she said next.

"Don't stop!" she whimpered. "Please, don't stop."

My body tightened with my impending release. I sank the fingers of my left hand into Candi's sweat-soaked hair and slid my right hand beneath her. Using my grip on her hair, I pulled her back against me. It was awkward due to our height difference, but I managed to stoop low enough to press my mouth to the curve of her neck.

I brushed my right hand up along her abdomen until it teased across her breasts. Candi arched her back, pushing her chest into my hand, and sobbed as she climaxed. Her body trembled in my arms and quivered around my erection, sending me over the edge and plunging into the abyss of ecstasy.

Yanking her head to the side to give myself better access, I sank my fangs into the smooth skin of her neck, claiming her as mine to love.

Chapter Fourteen

—CANDI—

My body was nothing more than a puddle of love-drunk goo by the time Aspen released me. The cool granite counter felt incredible against my flushed skin. I wanted to roll over and look at Aspen, but I was fairly sure my muscles had given up the ghost and moved on to the afterlife.

"Aspen, your balls are touching the counter!" Frost gagged. "I'm never eating anything that touches the island again. Scratch that! Let's just burn it. While we're at it, maybe we can burn the image of your hairy butt going to pound town out of my mind. Now that you're slightly more stable and I can trust you not to accidentally eat our mate, and not in a good way, I'm going to take a walk to clear my head."

Frost threw me a wink as he walked briefly into my line of sight on his way out the door. I tried to laugh over Frost's dramatics, but all that came out was a soft huff. My body was too exhausted to even manage a real laugh.

Frost's over-the-top craziness roused Aspen from the trance he seemed to be stuck in. My giant of a mate carefully scooped me off the counter, cradling me against his chest. Through heavy-lidded eyes, I gave him a sleepy smile. Instead of returning the smile, his jaw clenched, and tight lines appeared around his eyes as he took in my tired form.

"I'm so sorr—" Aspen began, voice hoarse.

"Stop," I whispered, pressing my palm against his mouth. "If you are about to apologize for what we just experienced, I don't want to hear it because that means you won't do it again, and you had better do that again."

Lifting his hand, he curled his fingers around my hand. Aspen placed a tender kiss on my palm before pulling my hand from his mouth so he could speak. "I love you, Candi Cane."

It was as though these men were gluing my damaged heart back together. The cracks and scars would always be there, but my heart was whole.

Aspen didn't give me time to respond. He moved up the stairs, carrying me straight to Coal's larger-than-life bed and placing me on it.

"No. I need to clean up first." My face burned with embarrassment as I realized how sticky I was.

"Hush, little wolf. Your body needs rest." Aspen disappeared into the bathroom.

The sound of water running drifted from the open doorway, and when Aspen returned, he held a towel in his hand. Sitting on the edge of the bed, I suddenly felt shy. I clamped my trembling legs together and pulled the corner of the sheet over my bare breasts.

The giant wolf dropped to his knees in front of me. "Don't hide your beautiful body from me." Ignoring my belated attempt at modesty, Aspen gently pried my legs apart.

His low whine of distress had me glancing down. A small smudge of blood was smeared on my inner thigh. I was honestly surprised there wasn't more. This was only my second time being with a man, and Aspen took huge to a whole new level.

"I hurt you." Aspen's voice shook.

"Yeah, and it felt incredible." I brushed my hand along his jaw, wondering if it was too soon to do it again.

"I should have been stronger and fought against my wolf's instincts," Aspen growled, his face twisting into disgust. "Why didn't you stop me? Why didn't I stop me?"

I growled right back at him. "Aspen, you warned me what was going to happen. You kept your wolf back long enough to give me a chance to decide what I wanted. And I wanted you. I don't regret that decision, and you better not regret our first time together."

Aspen didn't say anything else. Picking up the warm wet towel, he took his time cleaning up the evidence of our passionate lovemaking.

There was nothing sexual in Aspen's touch as he cared for me, but his nearness had my heart beating like a *drummer drumming.* Unable to resist peeking, I shot a glance at his thick member and wished I had the energy to put it in my mouth and play it like a *piper piping.* If my body hadn't already been pushed past the normal threshold for fatigue, I'd have been *a-leaping* on him. Yep. I'd have my way with him, while wiggling on his lap like a tipsy *lady dancing.* I sighed. It wasn't fair. How was I supposed to resist him when his body was *made for milking?*

"Goddess sake! Are you finished? Is this what your mind is always like?" Aspen stared at me in open-mouthed admiration. Or was that horror? His lip quirked up. "Admiration."

What a perfectly awful moment for the mental bond between us to grow strong enough for him to listen to my thoughts. Before I could help myself, I blurted out, "I was just thinking how I'd love to have your *sperms-a-swimming...*"

Aspen didn't let me finish. His lips captured my mouth in a searing kiss that made me forget all about the twelve days of Christmas and imagine lying around in his arms all day.

My eyes drifted closed, and my body slumped toward him. Aspen caught me, easily lifting me onto the bed and tucking me beneath the covers. I yawned and scooted against his chest. There was just one more thing I needed to do before I enjoyed a midmorning nap.

My sharp canines pierced Aspen's skin. *Mine.*

I SLEPT until the late afternoon sun cast shadows across the bedroom floor. The room felt like a sauna, and my hair stuck to my face. I tried to kick off the blanket to get some air, but I was stuck between two eight-packs of chiseled male muscles. My eyes darted between the two sets of delicious-looking abs and, unable to help myself, I gave a quick lick up the tanned chest to my right.

"Did you just lick me?" Coal's eyes opened to narrow slits.

"Um, yes?" I hesitated. "You looked yummy."

Plus, I was pretty much living out a real-life wet dream with these gorgeous men. It would be a shame not to fully appreciate it. I didn't add that bit out loud, but both men must have been in my head because they chuckled.

"Where's Frost?" I asked, not seeing him in the room.

"He's working on a project or something, but should be back soon." Coal pulled me against his chest.

Aspen pressed in tighter against my back, squishing me between their much larger bodies.

Coal nuzzled my neck. "Since you got to taste me, I think it's only fair I get a taste too." His tongue slid down my neck and disappeared between my breasts.

Not to be left out, Aspen licked and kissed a line down my spine. "Delicious little Candi Cane."

My mind short-circuited as Aspen and Coal continued

to lavish attention on my skin. I'm pretty sure I know what would have happened next if the door hadn't flown open and slammed against the wall.

"Nope. If anyone's getting a turn, it's me. But she needs to be fed and hydrated before I get my chance. Have you guys never had a pet? This is basic care." Frost grabbed my ankles and yanked me down the bed. "Come on, Pest. I have a plate of spaghetti and garlic breadsticks waiting for you downstairs." Flipping me over his shoulder, Frost strode toward the door.

Coal and Aspen protested my kidnapping, but Frost only responded with a middle finger salute before his hand slid over my butt.

The moment the earthy fragrance of roasted garlic tickled my nose, my stomach growled loudly.

"My poor little mate. I leave for a few hours, and they can't even remember how to take care of you," Frost mumbled, depositing me in a chair.

I rolled my eyes hard enough that I thought they might get stuck. "You know I'm an adult, right? I do have a general understanding of how to keep myself alive."

"Of course you do, but it's our job now." Frost gave me a gentle kiss on the lips before pulling back and sliding the plate of food in front of me.

Boy, did this guy know the way to a girl's heart!

I scarfed the whole thing in, like, three minutes flat while Frost gave a satisfied smirk. I'd just finished swallowing my last bite when Coal came down the stairs, cell phone in hand. "I just got a call from the Elder. He said the rest of the Elders showed up in Evergreen a few minutes ago. They are asking to meet you, and he wanted to know if you'd be willing to make the trip to see them this evening?"

I had to have misheard him. "ALL the Elders are in Evergreen?" The Elders never traveled as a group to visit a pack. Dread turned the food in my stomach to lead. I doubted this was good news for me.

"Yes, the Elder spoke with them about our situation, and they decided it was best to travel here in person." Coal ran a hand through his hair, giving away the fact he was worried, too.

I took a deep breath. "Tell him we will head that way in a few minutes. Let's get this out of the way, otherwise, I'm just going to sit around and worry."

Coal gave a sharp nod and typed some numbers into his phone as he headed back upstairs.

Pushing to my feet, I rinsed my plate off in the sink and placed it in the dishwasher. I trudged up the staircase, only to bump into Frost at the top.

"I thought you might need these." Frost held out several shopping bags.

I peeked inside to find jeans, several acid-washed T-shirts, and some bits of string and lace that I assumed were supposed to function as undergarments that were clearly picked out by a man who wanted to take them off. My eyes teared up at his thoughtfulness. He was the jokester who seemed to take nothing in life seriously, but he'd been watching and trying to anticipate my needs.

"Hey, hey! If they aren't your style, we can return them. Please don't cry." Frost's thumb wiped at a hot tear streaking down my cheek.

"I love them." I threw my arms around him. "Thank you, Frost."

He whispered, "Go get ready, Pest. Let's get this over with." Frost's tongue traced the curve of my ear. "I'm still waiting for my turn to be claimed, and I'm barely holding it together."

Swatting my butt, he pushed me down the hall. I wore a goofy grin while getting ready, and it stayed on my face right up until we crossed onto Evergreen's land.

Chapter Fifteen

—CANDI—

We pulled up in front of the main house, and I fought back the urge to throw up. I was the Evergreen Alpha. This was my pack. But I doubted I'd ever be able to look at the house I'd grown up in without being haunted by memories.

"We can burn it down," Coal offered.

I snapped my head to the driver's seat to check if he was joking. He wasn't.

"We can't just set fire to a perfectly good house!" I squeaked.

Coal pinned me with his cool, calculating gaze. "Why not? If seeing it is going to make you sad, it needs to burn."

"Because—well, because you just can't." I gave a nervous laugh. It was sweet, but a little crazy-sounding, too. "Are you going to go around burning down everything that makes me sad?"

"Yes." Coal tilted his head slightly, studying me. "I'll set the world on fire if that's what I need to do."

He was dead serious. I caught a glimpse of the alpha everyone feared and whispered about. Of course, instead of being scared, it turned me on.

"I'd help," Aspen added, reaching for the door handle.

"I'd bring the gasoline." Frost's blue eyes sparkled. "And I'd be sure to bring smores for you to snack on."

How could they be sweet but terrifying at the same time? And why did I feel so safe with them?

"Because we're your mates," Aspen answered simply and climbed from the SUV.

Coal brushed his fingers through my loose blonde hair. "There's nothing in this world or the afterlife I wouldn't do for you. You are mine—"

"Ours." Frost coughed.

Coal shot him an annoyed look. "Fine. Ours." Turning back to me, his voice dropped to a husky pitch that could rival the bass at a frat party. "The world may see you as an insanely powerful alpha, but never forget when the doors are closed, you belong to us. Mind, soul, and body, you are ours to protect and please. And that is something we are deadly serious about."

Aspen opened my door. "Alpha. Ready to lead the way?"

Nodding, I fought back my tears over my mates' complete devotion to me. Stepping out of the vehicle, I lifted my chin and headed toward the house, drawing strength from the three alphas walking a step behind me.

"You guys don't have to walk behind me," I hissed over my shoulder.

Cheshire grins spread across all three faces.

"We don't mind. The view is incredible." Frost winked.

I didn't have a chance to respond before the screen door opened, and my father—Kristof, stepped out. The moment I saw his face, my anxiety skyrocketed.

Watch him closely. I know that smile. He is going to try to distract us with fake jovialness, but he's planning something, I warned Aspen and Coal through the link, knowing they would pass the warning to Frost.

I still needed to learn how to delve into their minds like they did mine, but having never experienced the mental link before our mating, I was still adjusting to the new ability. The men had been using a mental link for years, so it came far more easily to them.

"We've built a fire in the pit outback. The Elders are waiting for you back there." Kristof came down the stairs with a bounce in his step that had alarms blaring in my mind.

There was no way my power-hungry father would so easily step down from the alpha position so easily, nor would he be so cheerful about it. Regardless of what he'd said to the Elder in Coal's house about honoring their judgment, he had no plans to allow me full control.

Coming around the side of the house, the backyard came into view. There was a fire blazing, but the yard was empty. A chill raced down my spine, warning me a split second before a wolf slammed into me, its jaws snapping at my throat.

No. Not my throat... He was aiming for Coal's mark on my neck. Randolph was trying to claim me by force.

"SHIFT!" I screamed the order, pushing the full force of my alpha command into it.

Randolph shifted faster than I'd ever seen a wolf shift before. He screamed as his bones broke and snapped from the speed of the shift, quickly forming themselves back into a human's form. His shift took less than three seconds to complete, but I suspected it felt much longer to the pile of reindeer turds in front of me.

To my shock, even through the pain, Randolph remembered his mission. He flung himself at my neck a second time, canines flashing. Let's be real. There was a far higher probability I'd catch a naked Coal singing Jingle Bell Rock while jingling his bells, than Randolph ever had of sinking his fangs into my neck.

My hair whipped wildly around my face as Coal blurred past me to catch Randolph around the neck. As though he weighed nothing, Coal lifted the beta's feet from the ground and blurred them both into the empty backyard.

Except it wasn't empty anymore. The Elders must have heard my shout or Randolph's screams because they'd emerged from the house onto the back porch. I noticed quite a few of the pack members had drifted toward the yard as well, their curiosity getting the best of them.

"You were warned." Coal shoved Randolph into the

blazing fire, not seeming to notice or care that his own arm was on fire.

"Coal!" I sobbed.

There was a sharp snap as Coal broke Randolph's neck and dropped his lifeless body into the crackling fire.

Kristof roared. He stepped up behind me, locking his right arm around my neck. There was a flash of silver as the knife in his left hand arched toward my throat. "A she-wolf will never lead my pack."

Everything was happening at the speed of light, and my mind was struggling to keep up. There were a hundred things I should have done at that moment. Given an alpha command, cracked his nuts with a hard kick, shifted into my wolf and bit his arm. But instead, I froze just like I always had as a little girl.

The horrific sound of bones shattering was followed by a wet, squelching sound. Kristof's hold on my neck loosened, then fell away as his body dropped to the ground like a sack of coal.

My legs felt stiff as I turned to see what had happened.

Aspen was standing close behind me. Kristof's body lay on the ground between us. There was a gaping hole in his back. Lifting my eyes, I watched as Aspen unceremoniously dropped the ex-alpha's heart to the ground and wiped his bloody palm down his jean-clad thigh. Because that was totally going to get his hand clean.

"He's dead?" I couldn't believe it.

Aspen didn't respond. His body vibrated like my father's death hadn't been enough to satisfy his bloodlust, and he couldn't figure out if he needed to be in human form or wolf.

Frost shoved a wolf away from him and rushed to me, sliding my back against his front. "Don't push me away right now."

I didn't. My relief at being free of my father was too great. I'd been worried he would spend the rest of his retired life following my every step and trying to bully me into doing things his way. Instead, he'd decided his title was more important than his own flesh and blood and tried to kill me.

The pack began to whisper, their words drifting through the yard.

It's the monster and his pack.

He's more terrifying than the stories make him out to be.

Do you think he's insane?

Why is he here in Evergreen?

Maybe he has rabies. Why else would he smile while burning himself?

I don't care if he has rabies. I'd let him infect me any day.

I snarled at the last comment, hot jealousy pushing me to put the female in her place. But it would have to wait until I was sure Coal was okay. Rushing to his side, I scanned his arm, expecting to find horrific burns. He was a wolf, so he'd heal, but extreme injuries like that could take weeks.

"How?" I whispered, running my fingers over the unmarred skin of his arm. The hair had been singed off, but the skin was completely uninjured.

Coal chuckled. "Fire doesn't affect me. Why do you think I became known as the Brimstone Alpha?"

The Elder who'd visited us this morning cleared his throat, drawing our attention to him. He nodded at Coal. "Coal."

Coal tilted his head. "Elder."

"Why would you take a werewolf's life in front of every Elder on earth?" a white-haired Elder demanded.

"Because I told him this morning that if he touched her again, he'd die. I keep my word." Coal's voice was flat.

How was he so calm when I was internally freaking out that they might take him from me or kill him for killing a wolf?

An Elder with fluffy red hair groaned and dropped into a chair. "Why is it always you, Coal? Do you ever get sick of being called in front of us?"

Coal lifted one shoulder in a shrug. "I thought you called me because you missed my cheery attitude." It was a statement so like Frost that I blinked a few times to make sure Coal was the one who'd said it.

A dark-haired Elder's shoulders shook, and he covered his mouth to hide his laughter.

"Do you know how much paperwork we will have to do because of these two idiots?" the red-haired Elder snapped. "At least Aspen's kill is open and shut. Kristof was going to murder Candi, and killing a mate is punishable by death, anyway."

"Are you going to arrest me and waste time since we all know you're going to let me go anyway, or should we go in and talk about why you're all gathered here?" Coal asked, resting his palm on the small of my back and guiding me toward the porch.

"You know we aren't going to arrest you. It's not worth the trouble," the Elder from this morning grumbled as we all moved into the house.

"And they're scared of you," the dark-haired Elder added, his eyes twinkling.

"Good. Just the way I like it." Coal chuckled and slapped a hand on the Elder's shoulder.

So it seemed that the rumors of the Brimstone Alpha hadn't been exaggerated as much as I'd thought.

If you'd known, would you have come down my chimney and stolen my heart? Coal's voice was a sensual brush against my mind.

I didn't even have to think about the answer.

Absolutely.

Chapter Sixteen

—CANDI—

We turned onto the long, winding road leading to the Brimstone house just before dawn. The logical thing would have been to stay in Evergreen. After all, the main house had plenty of room for the Elders and my mates, but my wolf refused to settle down while we were still in the house. It might be mine now, but it still felt like *his*.

We'd spent hours discussing the future of Evergreen, and my duty as the new alpha. The Elders had given me the option of stepping down and having a new alpha appointed. I considered it, but when I looked around at the familiar faces I'd grown up with, I saw hope. There wasn't a single teary eye in the room. They were relieved Kristof was dead.

I realized I wasn't the only one who'd been hurt by my father's selfishness. We all deserved a new start, and I was determined to do my best and not abandon the wolves who were trusting me to guide and protect them.

The Elders had also wanted to talk to me privately. I'd carefully blocked my mates from that conversation, but I was going to have to find a way to casually let them know my life was probably never going to be normal.

Exhausted and needing some quiet, I'd tried to think of a polite way to excuse myself from the Elders and the members of my pack who were scattered around the room. I shouldn't have worried. Coal took care of it by telling everyone he had matters to attend to in Brimstone that also required his luna. He'd gathered me in his arms and, with a curt nod, went straight out to our SUV, with Frost and Aspen on his heels.

I smiled, my head resting against Frost's shoulder as I thought of Coal making himself look like the arrogant butt-hole, so I didn't have to admit to my anxiety.

"He is an arrogant donkey's arse." Aspen's Scottish brogue was thicker when he was tired, and I wanted to listen to him talk for hours.

"I have much better things I could do to you for hours." Aspen's eyes glowed in the vehicle's dim interior, letting me see the feral hunger that lurked behind them.

"Back off." Frost flashed his fangs at Aspen. "I've stood by while you and Coal claimed our mate and created a bond, but my patience is running out."

At first, I thought he was messing with us, but his breathing was labored, and his blue eyes began to glow.

Aspen's muscles bunched, preparing to face off, but just

as quickly, he scooted back against the car door, giving Frost space.

Candi, Frost has always had the best control of his wolf. If he is struggling this much, it means he's under a lot of stress. It will help to calm him if you stay touching him and avoid touching Coal and myself until you two mate, Aspen said through the link while keeping his eyes focused out the windshield, as though ignoring me completely.

I put my hand on Frost's thigh and rested my head on his shoulder. For the next few minutes, we rode in tense silence. My brain kept going over and over the list of things I needed to do as Evergreen's new alpha. I'd set up an appointment to meet with some of the higher-ranking members of the pack. I would need a new beta, one I could trust.

"I could be your beta." Frost's breathing had calmed, and he almost sounded normal when he spoke.

Confused, I turned to face him. "You are Coal's beta! Then the Brimstone pack would need a new beta."

"Aspen can be Brimstone's Beta." Frost's answer came so fast, he had to have given this a lot of thought.

"Or..." Coal's eyes met mine in the rearview mirror. "I can step down as Alpha of Brimstone."

My jaw hit the floor. "And do what?" He was an alpha. The Alpha. Coal couldn't just walk away and live a normal —for a werewolf—life, could he?

"Be your luna, obviously." Frost snickered, his humor having returned. "I can already see him wearing those adorable aprons and making gingerbread houses with all the tourists."

Aspen's loud guffaw gave me the worst jump scare of my life. I yelped and nearly climbed into Frost's lap, and Coal accidentally slammed his foot on the brakes.

"Very funny." Coal tried to look annoyed, but he had trouble hiding his smile. "I'm serious, Candi. If you want to live in Evergreen, then I will step down and follow you."

The drive between the Evergreen and Brimstone houses took about two hours, and it took longer to run that distance on foot or in wolf form. I should know, having just done it myself. Biting my lip, I tried to decide whether I should tell them what I really wanted.

Yes, you should tell us. You're getting better at blocking your thoughts, and it's frustrating to only hear bits and pieces. I like listening to you, Aspen complained in my mind.

"What if…" I hesitated. This was a big ask. Maybe it was too much. We were fated mates, but we had only just met.

"Yes," Coal, Frost, and Aspen answered in unison.

"What?" I spluttered. "You guys don't even know what I wanted to ask! Plus, Frost can't hear my thoughts, so I'm sure he has no idea."

"Are you going to leave us?" Frost raised a brow, daring me to say yes.

"Of course not!" I protested.

Frost shrugged. "Then whatever it is, we're fine with."

Coal pulled the SUV to the side of the road and twisted around to give me his full attention. "We were tired of being lonely, but unable to change things. You fell into our lives and lit up that dark old house with just your presence. I've smiled more since that day than I've smiled in the last decade. I couldn't survive being plunged back into the darkness my life was before you. So yes. Yes to anything and everything that will allow me to wake up to your beautiful face every single day for the rest of our lives."

Tears ran down my cheeks, letting go of all the pain and hurt that I'd buried in my mind and heart since my mother died. I was loved. Truly loved.

Frost unbuckled my seatbelt and gathered me into his arms. He murmured what I thought were reassurances until my sobs quieted enough that I could actually hear his words. His voice was pitched low and soothing, but he was whispering pickup lines. Really, really stupid ones.

I couldn't help it, I laughed. Then I clutched his shirt, soaking it in happy tears.

"Well, are ye ever goin' to tell us what ye wanted to ask, lass?" Aspen's lilting brogue warmed my heart.

"Seriously, bro. Lay off the accent. It's an unfair advantage. You're lucky your parents let you spend so much time with your grandparents in Scotland growing up." Frost scowled at the Aspen. "And you're just laying it on thick because you figured out she thinks it's sexy."

"Would ye like tae take this matter outside, wee lad?" Aspen taunted.

Coal snorted as he pulled back onto the road. Frost pressed his hands over my ears and stuck his tongue out at Aspen.

He's forgotten I can talk to you without using my mouth.

Aspen's husky chuckle did something to my insides, and I was forced to clench my thighs together when I felt the tell-tale rush of heat.

Trying to distract the men, I answered Aspen, "I thought maybe we could build a house on the boundary line of our two territories. We would be more accessible to both packs that way."

Coal tossed his phone to Aspen.

Aspen tapped away at the screen for several minutes and then leaned forward to lay it on the armrest. "Done. They will be by tomorrow with sample blueprints and the best locations to build along the border for Candi to pick from. He is hiring two more crews, and it will be finished within three months."

"They start tomorrow? It will be finished within three months?" I asked, my heart thudding.

Maybe I wouldn't ever have to spend another night in the house that had been ruled by my father. I could commute between packs a few times a week until the house was finished.

"Yes. He's the best." Coal smiled at me in the mirror.

"Could he also build a guest house? I will use Evergreen money, so it won't cost you anything." I chewed on my lip, hoping I wasn't pushing my luck.

Coal nodded. "I don't see why not. We'll tell him to add it to the plans tomorrow. And there isn't a chance I'm letting my new little bride pay for her home. But why do you need a guest house?"

"It's for when Frost annoys her," Aspen whispered a bit too loudly.

"It's for the Elders." I decided to go ahead and drop the other bomb I'd been hiding from them in my mind. "We'll be seeing a lot of them since it turns out I'm the first female Elder. There have been other female alphas, but never one with three mates... and never one who could mark her mates or use an alpha command on another alpha. They had some old letters talking about a wolf who'd bring change to the werewolf species, but had chalked it up to a myth or parable. Boy, were they shocked to find out it was real."

That was true, but not nearly as shocked as I had been when they told me. The kind Elder I'd met this morning had grabbed me in a fatherly bear hug. He'd whispered that I was exactly what the wolves needed to change laws and create a better future.

"You're an Elder?" Frost had paled.

"Apparently." I patted his cheek. "But don't worry! I told them I didn't care if the moon goddess herself showed up at my doorstep, I wasn't leaving here. They could come to me or learn how to use Zoom."

The last ten minutes of the car ride were quiet, and I snuggled contentedly in Frost's arms. My gums ached with the need to drop my fangs and claim him, but I forced myself to fight the urge. Later. After he marked me.

We parked in front of the house, and Frost threw open the door and blurred into the house.

"What's going on?" I yelped, clinging to his shirt.

When Frost looked back down at me, his eyes glowed, and his fangs flashed. "If you think I didn't notice the scent of your arousal, you're dead wrong. It was all I could smell, and I barely kept myself from taking you right there in the car. But I can't wait anymore."

Chapter
Seventeen

—CANDI—

To my surprise, Frost took off at a sprint down the long hallway, hauling me tighter against his chest. I wrapped my legs around his waist, and my arms clutched at his neck to keep myself from falling. Coal and Aspen bellowed in outrage, followed by a crash and then thuds as they knocked over furniture in their quest to catch Frost.

Frost tore down the corridor, nearly crashing into a wall, and then took the stairs two at a time as he raced to stay ahead of the two angry, and probably horny, werewolves chasing us.

For the first time in what felt like years, I laughed. It wasn't just a giggle, either. No, this was the type of laugh that left you in tears and caused your sides to ache. It felt amazing. I didn't remember the last time I'd felt... happy.

Frost's chest rumbled as well, but not in laughter. This

was a growl that promised naughty things were in my near future. He leaned down and sucked my bottom lip into his mouth, sending instant heat flooding between my legs.

Coal and Aspen thundered up the stairs behind us. I clung tighter to Frost's neck, my laughter echoing in the narrow hall. Frost turned into a doorway and slammed the door closed behind us. He tossed me onto the bed and spun around to shove a dresser in front of the door as though it weighed nothing.

"That should slow them down." He chuckled and then dove onto the bed beside me, pulling me into his arms and kissing me voraciously.

The door shook as the men outside slammed into it. Loud banging followed. "Frost! This is not okay!" Coal's voice was muffled, but I could still hear the irritation. "Open the door now."

The full power of Coal's alpha tone dripped from the command, but Frost ignored it. "No. It's my turn to kiss our girl and make her scream. Go away," Frost responded, his mouth moving down my neck.

With a moan, I relaxed and stretched out along the length of his body. His lips found mine in a slow kiss. It was slow and sweet, as though there weren't two angry alphas loudly threatening how they were going to make it so Frost couldn't have children if he didn't open the door.

Frost's fingers dove into the now tangled mess of my hair, careful to not hurt me. He slowly rubbed my scalp. The gesture was soothing, but also caused my toes to curl.

My eyes drifted to the ceiling, and I blinked hard. "Is that mistletoe?"

Frost pulled back and smiled proudly. "Yep. I knew one kiss wasn't going to satisfy my hunger, so I figured I'd keep you busy in here for a while."

He wasn't kidding. This wasn't a single ribbon with a bit of mistletoe dangling from it. No, this crazy man had covered the ceiling with an entire carpet of mistletoe.

For the first time since Frost had brought me into the room, I actually studied it. I knew this was his bedroom because it was the only scent I could pick up, which was good for him. My wolf and I weren't in the sharing mood. A Christmas tree stood in one corner, sparkling with gold and silver ornaments. Christmas lights twinkled where they had been strung around the room. The room even smelled of Christmas, with the spicy-sweet scents of gingerbread, cinnamon, and cloves.

"You did this for me?" I whispered.

Frost brushed a finger across my cheek. "Yes. It's why I left the house for a little while yesterday. I thought you might get homesick, and I wanted to make at least one room of the house feel a little more familiar. It's silly."

"No, it's not silly. It's romantic. I love you, Frost." I pulled his face to mine for a kiss.

The door groaned, rattling in its frame, but as far as we were concerned, it was just the two of us left on earth. I didn't miss his slight smirk at some of the more creative curses coming from the hallway, though. He slowly pulled my clothing off, his eyes drinking in every inch of skin he exposed.

Leaning back over me, Frost's hand moved to the small of my back, tucking me closer. My temperature climbed right along with my desire, and my wolf howled in my mind, eager to complete the claim with our unmarked mate. By the time Frost's hand found its way to the apex of my thighs, I was breathing hard.

I growled in frustration when his hand disappeared before he'd even touched my aching heat. Rolling me onto my back, Frost tossed off his shirt and leaned down to nuzzle my neck. He was careful to keep his weight over his shoulders and not crush me. "I'm hopelessly in love with you."

I looped my arms around his neck. Drawing him close, I nipped his earlobe and teased. "I kinda like you, too. But I'd like you more if you were inside me."

My fingers traced along the carved indentions of his muscles. Werewolves in general were ripped, but Frost took it to a whole different level.

His hand found my breast, teasing the hard peak of my nipple. My heart stumbled before finding its rhythm and then losing it again. When he captured my breast in the heat of his mouth, I nearly died on the spot. Pure ecstasy rocked through me, pleasure shooting through my body like lightning.

I clutched at his broad shoulders, my nails leaving light scratch marks across his skin. Frost devoured one breast and then the other, his tongue curling and working to drive me wild.

I writhed beneath him, beyond desperate for friction. Unable to stop myself, I wrapped my legs around his tight waist and ground myself against him.

Frost groaned as his throbbing erection pressed against my slit, with only his pale gray jogging pants between us. His eyes glazed over with need as he rocked against me.

"I need you." The words were growled through his clenched teeth, and the low tone vibrated through my insides.

Slipping my thumbs into the waistband of his pants, I slid the material over his hips. As more of his body came into view and his erection sprung free, there was only so much I could do to not drool. With a loud groan, Frost kicked off the pants before positioning himself over me again.

I couldn't resist. Taking his erection in my hand, I gently ran my fingers along his impressive satin length. He expelled his breath in a slow hiss. "I can't wait anymore, Candi."

Unable to find words, I simply nodded and hoped my eyes told him what my words could not. I guided him to my slick entrance, sucking in my breath as he pushed himself in, inch by inch. It was my turn to hiss as he stretched me past what was comfortable. Frost's body was stiff as he forced himself to go slow and give me time. Each time I thought there was no more room, he would push in further.

I groaned, the sound a mix of pain and pleasure. My mind was overloaded with the intensity of the sensations, and I forced myself to remember to focus on breathing. Frost wasn't as thick as Aspen, but he was definitely longer. Once he was completely sheathed inside me, he paused, allowing me to catch my breath. I could feel him jerk against my sensitive walls.

"Please," I finally managed to speak. "Make me yours."

Frost didn't have to be told twice. With a gentleness that melted my heart, he slid out of me. When he had almost pulled himself free, he began a slow stroke back in. I expected Frost to get rough, like it had been with Coal and Aspen, but he kept a steady pace, taking his time and making sure my walls adjusted to his length.

Half of me wanted to scream at him to go faster, but the other half loved the way he took his time. The man was covering me in kisses and worshipping my body... and I was here for it.

My body thrummed, my need building and pushing me toward the brink. Frost continued his steady, rhythmic pace that was building a powerful need inside me. It felt like a tsunami was headed my way, and I could do nothing but watch.

Frost nuzzled my neck, his wolf preparing to leave his permanent mark. I turned my head, giving him better access and longing to feel his fangs pierce my skin.

Sweat soaked our bodies as Frost built the need inside us into a raging inferno, all while continuing to thrust inside my velvet heat at the same tender pace.

"Frost, I'm going to—" My breath came in gasps, my need becoming something primal inside me.

Frost's canines sank into the skin of my neck as he thrust hard into me, burying himself deep. My release exploded from inside me. I tried to scream, but the exquisite pleasure stole the breath from my lungs, and I fought to stay conscious.

Clinging to Frost's broad back, I sank my canines into his shoulder, my wolf marking him as forever mine. Frost roared his own release into my neck, the sound muffled with his teeth still embedded in my skin.

As the world came back into focus around us, I realized we weren't alone.

A slow clap drew my attention to the small couch in the corner. Coal sat spread out on the couch, heat simmering in his eyes as he clapped dramatically. Aspen sat on the floor, the fly on his jeans undone and one leg drawn up as he stroked his stiff erection.

They looked like a spread in a men's magazine, and my wolf strutted in my mind, proud of her sexy-as-sin mates. Coal rose to his feet and stalked toward me, a predator hunting his mate.

To think, this had all started with me running from being hunted. And now, I was positively giddy at the mere thought of it. Oh, the irony!

"Aspen, how many more times do you think we can make her come apart before she begs for mercy?" Coal's voice was silken, all smoke and sex.

My body clenched in response.

"My record was four. I say we try to double that." Aspen rose to his feet, his eyes glowing.

Frost grunted as I shoved him away from me and leaped up from the bed.

I wanted these men… but they didn't have to know how badly I wanted them to catch me.

"Bring it on, wolfies!" With a squeal, I darted out the bedroom door and down the hallway.

Spoiler alert. I didn't get far.

Mating hunts might not be so bad after all.

ABOUT SEDONA ASHE

Sedona Ashe doesn't reserve her sarcasm for her books; her poor husband can tell you that her wit, humor, and snarky attitude are just part of her daily life. While she loves writing paranormal shifter reverse harem novels, she's a sucker for true love, twisted situations, and wacky humor.

Sedona lives in a small town at the base of the Great Smoky Mountains in Tennessee. She and her husband share their home with their three children, adorable pup, five cats, two pet foxes, chickens, three crazy turkeys, two cows, and over a hundred reptiles.

When she isn't working, she enjoys getting away from the computer to hike, free dive, travel, study languages, and capture the essence of places and people in her photography. She has a crazy goal of writing one million words in a year and spending six months exploring Indonesia.

Made in United States
Troutdale, OR
12/12/2023

15696739R00099